PROM
Impossible

Laura Pauling

Redpoint Press
Prom Impossible
Copyright 2014 Laura Pauling
All rights reserved

Summary: Cassidy knows that Michael Greenwood is
her one true love—he just doesn't know it yet. She spends
her senior year helping him figure that out in time for prom,
but instead, she comes close to losing her true identity, her
friends, and the chance at the real thing that's right in front
of her.

Edited by A Little Red Inc.
Cover design by Laura Pauling and Steven Novak

ISBN-13: 978-1499737776
ISBN-10: 1499737777

Visit http://laurapauling.com

Also by Laura Pauling

CIRCLE OF SPIES

A Spy Like Me

Heart of an Assassin

Vanishing Point

Twist of Fate

Heist

The night my life changed forever.

SMOKE BILLOWED OUT THROUGH the side doors of the high school gym in great puffy clouds, creating exactly the effect we'd wanted. It filled the night sky with the sweet—okay, the smoky—scent of revenge.

At the time, we were juniors. The underclassman. The underdogs. And my cousin, Jules, was in an all out war with the senior class queen bee. We'd endured a year of lost battles, detentions at failed pranks, and lies, thanks to Bea Wallace.

It was senior prom, and it didn't take long for everyone to stampede into the parking lot. Flashes of brightly colored dresses appeared through the smoke, the girls panicking and the guys pretending they were all macho and protective when they were probably peeing their pants. We just set up a few strategically placed smoke blasters to add a little excitement to their lives. Stories to tell their grandchildren. In a few years they'd be thanking us and laughing about it all.

The whole idea had started when my Uncle Rudie and Dad sent the grilled pizza up into flames. I'm not even sure who came up with it first, but suddenly Jules and I were planning revenge with words like prom and smoke machines sneaking into the conversation.

We didn't even debate. There was no doubt. We knew we'd settle the score the night of senior prom as our way of saying goodbye and good riddance.

The fire trucks zoomed into the parking lot faster than we'd expected, their lights flashing and sirens blaring.

The smoke in the air tickled my nose and back of my throat. "Um, do you think what we did could be considered more than a prank? Like a felony? Maybe we used one too many blasters."

"No way. It's just smoke, Cassidy." Jules peered around the corner of the building.

Firemen stormed the side lawn and rushed into the gym with gas masks and hoses at the ready. A sickening feeling in the pit of my stomach mushroomed into the need to puke behind the bushes.

I nudged Jules and couldn't help but glance at the trail through the woods that led to our getaway. "We really should get going. I'll go start the car..."

Nothing I said would've changed her mind. She was set in her spot behind the landscaping, her eyes fixed on the parking lot in hopes of finding Bea.

"Just a few more seconds," she finally whispered back.

My skin prickled and my armpits were sticky and uncomfortable. A sure signal I needed to leave. "I'll see you back at the car."

"Uh-huh." She was still fixated.

I stepped out from behind the bush, my feet itching to run.

"Stop right there, miss," the deep voice called from the shadows.

Mistake one? I didn't stop. The heat of getting caught flared and my armpit sweat morphed from a trickling stream into a river. Slowly, I moved toward the woods while spitting out the planned excuses. I held out my chemistry book. "Just getting my chem book for finals, officer, sir."

"Stop. Now." His voice grew deeper and more threatening.

My getaway slowed to a crawl. I waved the thick text. "Got to get studying."

I glanced at the woods. What if I outran him to the waiting car and we ended up in a high-speed chase through the neighborhood? All I could picture were the explosions and fire and flipped over cars that usually ended those chases. I didn't want to end up like that.

It was almost our senior year. I was too young to die.

"Hands up!" the cop ordered.

Slowly, I turned and raised my hands with the heavy text. Why hadn't we picked English Lit so I could hold up a slim copy of poetry?

I didn't even give the cop a chance to ask any questions. I produced a few crocodile tears, which wasn't hard, because I was in complete panic mode.

"Oh, please, sir, I'm just trying to achieve high grades. My senior year is coming up and that means college applications."

"You had nothing to do with this?" He nodded toward the fleeing prom couples.

"That's the truth, sir." My voice came out shaky like I was about to break down.

"Then I guess you won't mind coming down to the station and taking a polygraph while chatting with the detective."

This was where I realized I watched too many crime shows and interrogations where the cops shouted and played mind games. I blurted out the truth.

"Okay, yes, I lied. I'm sorry. I panicked and cops scare me." His face steeled like I was in for it. "I appeal to your softer side, officer. Maybe you have kids and know they make mistakes. I've made mistakes but I've seen the light." He narrowed his eyes and reached for the handcuffs on his belt—or was it his gun? I blubbered. "I'm not perfect, I admit, but please don't throw me in jail for years. My parents will kill me. They said one more thing and my life would be over."

"One more thing?" He raised an eyebrow and his face softened. Maybe there was a slight chance.

"It really wasn't my fault when our storage shed burst into flames or when the fire alarm at the mall went off or when the entire ski lodge had to be evacuated on our vacation. Seriously. I swore I saw someone sneak a homemade bomb into the trashcan. It turned out to be trash but it looked suspicious and we'd just had a bomb threat at school so I had bomb on the brain. They were all innocent mistakes. You can see that, right, sir?"

That was when I realized that what I mistook for compassion was really an amused curiosity. I should've stuck to the story. Thank God I didn't mention all our failed pranks this past year. That definitely would've made me look guilty.

"Why don't we take a little ride and you can explain your story down at the station. With your parents."

"Oh."

I tried not to wiggle when his hand clamped down on my arm like I was a threat to humankind. I didn't look back once because Jules and I had made a pact that if one got caught, the other wouldn't squeal.

I just never thought the one getting shoved into the back of squad car would be me.

MY PARENTS ARRIVED AT the station with unusually pale complexions. Mine probably wasn't any better. I'd hoped for some comfort food like cupcakes or homemade chocolate chip cookies. Even bakery cookies would do in a pinch. But no such luck.

They listened. They nodded their heads, but I didn't see even one fake smile, for me anyway. They uh-huhed and yessed and said "We completely understand" a lot.

The drive home was silent and scary. Dad finally spoke when we were in the driveway.

"We'll need time to talk to the school and think about this so we don't make any rash decisions. Make no mistake. We are disappointed in your decision, and there will be consequences."

That was all that was said for weeks.

CHAPTER 1

As THE WEEKS PASSED, I focused less on smoky proms and rides in police cars and more on Michael Greenwood, the boy destined to become my soul mate and my date to senior prom the next spring.

Jules crouched next to me in the scratchy bushes outside of Michael's house. Lately, she'd been extra nice. Total guilt complex. I wasn't complaining.

Only two people knew about my love for Michael: Jules and my brother, Carter. He guessed it from my swoony expressions over certain heart doodles in my room. Talk about nosy. And Jules knew from the very start because for years we'd been more than just cousins. We were best friends even though she was slightly more popular. Okay, a lot more.

She nudged me. "Spying on the biggest dork in school? That's the big emergency?"

"Hey, he's got potential. And I'm not spying. I'm observing the behavioral patterns of my future boyfriend."

She giggled. "Well, he might be kinda cute behind all the dorkiness. I'll give you that. And I've never had a chance to get to know him. Maybe he's cool."

I'd known Michael since he peed his pants the first day of kindergarten from pure nerves and the fear of asking how to find the bathroom. We'd been on and off friends and engaged in frequent conversations about Smaug, Aragorn as an alpha male, and Gollum's greatest moments.

We were destined to fall for each other with a passionate forever-kind-of-love. Someday, he'd take me in his arms and sweep me off my feet with the most romantic, passionate kiss in history.

"This is crazy," Jules whispered. Then in an act of complete betrayal, she grabbed some pebbles and pelted the downstairs window.

"What are you doing?" I jerked her arm away but it was too late.

"Helping you. I assumed that's why you called me. You said it was an emergency. You said you couldn't do it alone." She stood and brushed the dirt off her shorts. Before I could complain she hugged me. "You can do it, Cass. Good luck!"

A window slammed open.

"Who's there? I've got my death ray gun that can sizzle your brain in three seconds and I'm not afraid to use it."

"Oh. My. God." She stifled a laugh. "He's all yours."
And with that Jules shoved me into open view.

I stumbled forward, tripping and practically slamming into the side of the house. *Thanks, Jules.* "Hi, Michael. Fancy meeting you here."

"Oh, it's you. Hi, Cassidy. And I live here. Remember?"

I giggled. "That's right. I totally forgot. I was just out for an evening stroll—alone—to take in the beauty of nature and the glimmering stars in the velvet sky."

"Isn't that your cousin running away?" He squinted into the darkness. He was wearing his pointy ears again.

I peered into the trees. "I don't think so."

"Hmm. Could've sworn it was Jules." He shook his head, mumbling, and dropped into a chair in front of his computer. He blabbed on about some complicated algorithm that I tried to understand.

I nodded my head and said, "Sure." He took a breath before rambling on, so I jumped at the chance and spoke up. "Any plans for the summer?"

He almost seemed surprised I was still there. That's a sign of a great boyfriend. He was focused and attentive. I just needed to swing his focus my way. I fluffed my hair and let it dangle by my shoulders.

His eyes went back to the screen. "I've been working on this video game, and I hope to work on it all summer."

"Don't forget sun block," I teased.

"Huh?" He doesn't always get my sense of humor, especially when working.

"Never mind." One thing with boys is that you can't pester them too much or they'll be totally turned off and think you're a stalker. "Plan on hanging out by the pool?"

"Uh, yeah, sure."

"Trying to flirt with all the girls?" I hinted, hoping he'd say no.

He mumbled something and looked away. A rosy blush crept into his cheeks. He was playing naïve. Guys sometimes have trouble expressing their real emotions especially when they haven't admitted it to themselves.

Time to pull out the big guns, or I should say my death ray gun. I sighed and cleared my throat, glad that the dark would hide my reddening cheeks. In my best impersonation of Gollum, which was horrible, I said. "Sneaky little hobbitses."

He immediately perked up.

I continued, "Wicked. Tricksy. False."

He jumped right in. "No, not master."

Then I forgot the lines. "Um, precious ring. Want the ring. Need the ring!" I tried my hardest to get into the role that made me look cute and not like a freaky old guy with no hair. "Where's the ring? It must be here somewhere."

Michael huffed. "You messed it up."

I knew it! "Sorry." And I'd been practicing that for weeks. Thank God Jules had left or she'd never let me live this down. I decided it was time for me to leave.

"Well, better head back so the 'rents don't worry." After one sinful, heavenly moment, in which I imprinted his image into my mind, I slipped back into the night. "Bye."

"Bye."

I stepped to the side and listened. Seconds later, I heard the movie clips from YouTube. He cackled and continued with more voice impressions.

It was something about how he said bye—kind of soft, like a murmur. Yup. He definitely liked me. I wondered if I should leave an anonymous note with suggestions on how to ask a girl to prom—ones that didn't include voice impressions and pointy ears and laser guns that melted brains.

I bounced along the path back home on the wings of love. I walked into my house and joined my family for dinner, my heart all aflutter. When I was almost done with my second piece of garlic bread, I finally noticed my parents subtly glancing at me and then each other.

Uh-oh. I could sense the coming storm. My actions were about to catch up with me. I'd been hoping they forgot about last spring.

Time for an emergency butter-up-the-parents kind of talk. "So, I was thinking about asking Aunt Lulu to get me a job at the country club this summer. Get out in the fresh air for some good old-fashioned hard work. You know."

Dad coughed. "Hmm. We'll see."

"I even thought about putting in some volunteer work. Not just for purely altruistic reasons, but it would look great on the college applications. Right, Mom?"

"Possibly." She nodded, not committing to anything, but gave my dad the eye.

My suspicions were right.

Chapter 2

I COULDN'T TELL ANYONE that Jules had been the mastermind behind my brief dabbling in the criminal world.

But, secrets aren't *that* bad. In fact, they might even help out in the dating department, because secrets add that mysterious element that makes a guy want to know more. I can't explain how it happens. Just like I can't explain how whenever there's a new bag of chips in the house, I'm drawn to them, and then they're gone in twenty minutes. Or how I automatically wake up two minutes before Carter every morning and so get all the hot water in my shower. I mean, all he has to do is set his alarm.

After the quietest dinner in our history, my parents excused my twin brother, Carter, from the table and told him to read in bed. When he complained that his bedtime had never been 6:30, they gave him the look. The one that said *Remember our little talk we had about your sister?* After flashing me a sympathetic smirk—if there is such a thing—he headed upstairs.

My parents hemmed and hawed and fidgeted. In the time it took them to start and stop sentences and give each other looks, trying to get the other one to start, I could've knitted an ugly sweater for my Aunt Lulu. I can't knit well, but that doesn't matter, because Aunt Lulu would never wear it. I just like to see her squirm.

Finally, they ushered me into the living room. I settled onto the couch and pulled the ratty afghan over me, playing with the edges, trying to fight off an extreme case of the jitters.

Mom patted down loose strands of hair, smoothed her shirt, and reached for my dad's hand. Uh-oh. This was a united front, meaning I'd have almost no wiggle room for negotiations.

"Cassidy, we love you very much." A smile lit up her face. While Mom talked, Dad made sure to nod emphatically. "We've also noticed since our last talk how hard you've tried to reign in the impulsive actions."

This was where Mom paused to gather her nerves while the spaghetti and meatballs we ate for dinner did the cha cha in my stomach. At that moment, I truly regretted the triple-decker ice cream I pigged out on that afternoon.

Dad squeezed her hand and picked up the gauntlet. Kind of like a good cop/bad cop routine. "We're proud of you, Cassidy, and we have the highest hopes and know you'll be successful in life. After this coming summer, you'll be a senior, almost an adult, and your mom and I have a wonderful idea to help you on the road to success. We heard about—"

"I think I'm going to barf." I covered my mouth and made gagging noises. They told me they'd talk about the consequences and get back to me. Well, that moment had come, and I wasn't ready for it.

I ran to the bathroom upstairs, slammed the door so they'd think I was in there, then slipped into Carter's bedroom. Not that I didn't feel like puking because a big part of me did. Carter and I didn't always get along, but he's my twin, and a twin should always be there for the other one, even if there is no special mental connection. I mean, I had no idea about the time he snuck out of the house two years ago to meet up with his girlfriend, or the time he dented Mom's van and I got blamed.

I leaned against his door, my eyes closed, practicing the breathing techniques I'd learned for times like this when I was about to explode from a self-induced panic attack.

He gently strummed his guitar. He was trying to be the cool garage band guy with his own set of groupies. He could write love songs and the girls could swoon. "So they told you?"

I nodded, rolling my eyes and putting forth my best act to convince Carter I already knew my punishment. "Yeah. Totally stinks."

He stopped playing. "I hate to say I told you so."

"Please. That's not what I need right now." I flopped down on his bed, creating a ripple effect that blew his sheets of music to the floor. I caught a glimpse of Taylor Swift lyrics. "Seriously?" I stifled a laugh. "I don't think the girls are going to go for a guy singing Taylor Swift. You should pick something a little cooler."

"Shut up." He gathered up his music and shoved it into the folder. "It was free, okay?"

"Sure thing, bro." I gave him some time so he wasn't quite as annoyed with me. "Can you believe what they want me to do?"

He closed his guitar case. "Honestly? They surprised me. I thought they'd make you spend the summer cleaning out the garage and attic and doing random chores, but I never thought they'd..." He paused and studied me, his eyebrows lowering and he did this thing he does with his mouth when he knows he's being played.

Uh-oh. My brother is the one person in the world I have a hard time lying to. I guess we did have a special twin connection after all, just not the kind I wanted.

"You pulled the barf routine, didn't you?"

I played with his pillowcase fraying around the edges. "Maybe..."

My parents called from the bottom of the stairs. "Cassidy? We know you're up there." Then just in case I really did have to barf and they'd feel bad for not believing me, my mom said, "You feeling alright?"

They started up the stairs. I grabbed Carter's arm. "Help!"

He yanked away, clearly annoyed that I put him in the middle of this. "You're the one famous for getting out of scrapes, not me."

"At least tell me what they're going to say. I have to know."

He shrugged. "I can't tell you. They'd kill me."

Mom knocked on the bathroom door. "Cassidy? You ready to come back down?"

Carter must've have noticed the I'm-about-to-puke look that crossed my face, or he was scared I'd actually puke into his guitar. He'll do anything when it comes to preserving his image, and with a puke-scented guitar he wouldn't be roping in the chicks.

"Fine." He nodded toward the closet. I dashed into it and pulled the door shut just as Mom opened his door.

"Have you seen Cassidy?"

I should've accepted my fate and let my parents talk to me. Maybe it wasn't going to be as bad as I thought. It's not like hiding out with my brother's week-old socks and smelly T-shirts was helping.

Moments later, in what I consider the ultimate act of betrayal on my brother's part, Mom opened the door and I spilled out, a cheesy grin plastered on my face. "Oh, hi."

When Mom turned to go without even a word, just a look of complete and utter frustration, I flashed Carter a dirty glare. Then because I was ticked off, I stomped downstairs and slumped onto the couch. "Fine. I'm ready."

I guess their well of patience had runneth out, because they stopped trying to make this sit-down experience nice and sweet.

With straight shoulders and a blank face, Dad laid it all out. No messing around. "Cassidy, we've given you chance after chance and you just can't seem to get your act together. Frankly, we're done with all your crap." Except he didn't use exactly that last word.

Mom gasped. She has an allergy to swear words due to her church background. Any time something close to a swear slips out in her vicinity, Mom's face goes white and she acts all dizzy and has to fan her face. It's kind of embarrassing, especially when out in public and she says it loud enough so the offending party hears, and the offending party happens to be your possible future boyfriend's father. Just saying.

"It's okay," Dad said. "It's the truth." He turned all his seriousness toward me. "We're worried about you. It's like you don't have any moral guide or ruler to measure your actions up against."

Mom burst in, beaming, trying to make light of the situation like I just got invited to some amazing party or something. "You've been accepted to—"

"You're not sending me out to the extreme wilderness with just a water bottle and a loaf of bread where I get in trouble for pooping behind the wrong bush, are you?" I felt it coming on, a full-blown attack. The room spun, and my breathing sounded like a freight train in my ears.

My breath whooshed out, and I ducked my head between my knees. Mom was right beside me in two seconds, lovingly stroking my back and shushing me. "No, we'd never do that. You've been accepted to the Adventure Program at school for the summer."

"And you're grounded too," Dad added for effect.

All at once I thought about everything I'd miss. Hanging out with my friends, the pool parties, Michael. It was the summer before my senior year—and they were robbing me of the experience.

"It'll be okay. Your father and I felt like we had no other option but now that I think about it, maybe there are other ways..."

I let out a shudder. "I've heard about this program. They bore you so badly they suck the creativity right from your brain. Trouble makers from other schools come. What if they leave us unguarded and one of the kids tries to escape? And he uses me for a shield as he tries to force his way out with a plastic knife? Who knows what could happen to me?"

I used my controlled breathing and gave my parents room to consider the danger they were inflicting on me.

"Dear, she does have a point. Maybe we should consider all other options first."

I was so close to having everything I wanted that summer, except possibly cleaning out the garage. And honestly, in the heat of summer, that would truly be torture.

"Who will I leave my goldfish to if I die?"

The tension in the room skyrocketed and since my head was still between my knees, I couldn't interpret the silent communication. Turned out I didn't need to.

"Enough!" Dad roared. "Enough of your crap." Again, he didn't quite use that exact last word.

"Lord almighty, forgive him," Mom exclaimed.

"She's not having a panic attack. She probably never has. She's playing you just like she always has, and you're falling for it like always."

"You heard her breathing. Her face is pale. She almost got sick."

"Because she got in trouble and has to live with the consequences, that's why."

I lifted my head up just enough to catch a look at my dad's face. Sure enough, it was blistering red and veins bulging everywhere. Every few seconds, I spaced out my breathing until it sounded normal. Tears were hot against my eyelashes. I lifted my head and grabbed my dad's hands.

"Daddy, I'm sorry I disappointed you. I don't want you to hate me. I promise I'll never never *never* break another rule as long as I'm alive. I think I just need more prayer. Then I'll be the daughter you've always wanted."

His words were soft and fell over me like a light sprinkle of rain on a hot summer day. "Cassidy, you are the daughter I've always wanted."

I hugged him, knowing that I'd never feel as accepted and loved as I did at that moment. I peered at him through my tears. "Then I can see my friends?"

"Unfortunately, no. Seems like the Lord would have other plans for you. The program starts the day after tomorrow."

CHAPTER 3

SLEEP IS THE BEST WAY to procrastinate, and the next day, I procrastinated all afternoon.

I awoke to the tantalizing smell of my favorite meal, grilled cheese sandwiches with tomatoes. Mom did feel guilty. I stumbled down the stairs to my entire family.

My parents must've thought this was a grand idea: schedule a party with extended family, so I couldn't break them down and change their minds.

I stood at the bottom of the stairs, staring at the smiling faces of my family and friends. The forced looks of innocence like they didn't know what was really going on.

Uncle Rudie patted his big belly like he was pregnant or possibly thinking of the twenty grilled cheese sandwiches he planned on chowing down. Aunt Lulu flicked the top of his hand as if to punish him for the subconscious act. He flashed her a look of annoyance, then smiled sweetly and murmured something to her. Aunt Lulu nodded then went back to her smug look while she studied me.

I don't know why or how my mom can possibly be sisters with my Aunt Lulu. They're different as night and day. Aunt Lulu is like a tornado and my mom is the quiet after the storm. For a moment—just a small, itty-bitty moment—I appreciated my mom.

Jules stood in the corner with Elena. With her blonde hair perfectly pulled back in a high ponytail, Jules looked the vision of a perfect daughter. She'd look beautiful in a brown paper sack, so it didn't help that Aunt Lulu treated her like a show poodle.

It struck me that no one would ever guess she was my partner in crime. For some reason that idea didn't sit well in my stomach. But a pact is a pact.

With her arms crossed, she gave me a look that said, *the backyard ASAP*. She whispered something to Elena—probably along the lines of "Stay here while I talk to Cassidy about her six-week long imprisonment."

Elena lived nearby and we'd been best friends in elementary school, but over the course of growing up and middle school, we'd drifted apart. We were friends. We just didn't share anything too personal like crushes and soul mates.

Mom whooshed into the room like a tsunami, a tray balanced delicately on her shoulder, glasses of wine already teetering precariously. She gave everyone round two.

I boldly strode across the room and plucked a glass from the tray when her back was turned. Flipping around, I banged into Dad, his eyebrows almost touching his nose. I handed him the glass. "Here, Dad. Thought you might be thirsty."

"Thank you. What a *thoughtful* daughter I have." He steered me toward the kitchen. "Soda is in the kitchen."

"Gee, thanks." And don't think for one second, I didn't notice his emphasis on the word thoughtful.

In the kitchen, Carter popped open a root beer and joked with Jasper, who fell in the category of guys I call the jerky jocks. They were beautiful and they knew it, and I tried my best not to talk to any of them even though they were in my circle of friends, kinda. My brother slurped down his soda, eyeing me.

I let my fingers run along the counter where I sit every morning with a cup of hot chocolate. It's the best spot because the sun streams through the window, and it's warm.

Carter leaned into me. "Instead of wasting your time mad at Mom or Dad maybe you should be eating your last meal. I heard they're cutting sugar from your diet." He pulled back. "Just sayin'."

"Thanks for the tip." As soon as he and Jasper waltzed out of the kitchen, probably thanking God above that they weren't me, I grabbed a large fruit bowl, the kind

Mom uses for special casseroles and potluck dinners. I raided the cupboards, the pantry, the fridge, and swiped a whole tray of appetizers, then with it all balanced on my arms, I kicked open the back door and sneaked into the backyard.

I settled into the lounge chair on the patio.

The screen door squeaked again. Jules slipped outside, her shimmery skirt see-through with the kitchen light behind her. Her flowing flowery tank whispered against her hips like she was some kind of goddess.

She plopped down next to me in the matching wicker rocker. "What are you eating?"

"The last supper?" I shoved the rest of a pickle into my mouth, the juice running down the sides of my chin. After that I chose the little wieners wrapped in croissants, the macaroni salad, graham crackers, and cherry tomatoes.

She wrinkled her perfect little nose, tilted at just the right angle, so it was cute instead of snout-like. I spent years in middle school wanting her nose. I tried pushing and prodding, hoping that with enough force my nose would tilt like hers. It didn't work.

"Disgusting." After she spoke, she became fascinated with her pink and silver nail polish starting to chip.

"Looks like it's almost time for a new coat." My words came out muffled due to the cold sausage and pepper pizza I was wolfing down.

She nodded. "Mom said the same thing." She continued to pick, the flakes falling to the stone like dandruff. "Cassidy?" Her voice was all broken up. She picked harder, the paint coming off in bigger flakes.

"You must be excited for the big summer before senior year. You'll rule the pool at the country club. Make sure to take lots of pictures. Maybe make a flat cardboard version of me and take pictures, so I can pretend." I only stopped talking to finish off the crust and start on the fudge nut ice cream, which was starting to melt.

"You don't have to make me feel guilty." She lifted her face, the sun beams cascading across her cheekbones and glistening on her lip gloss. Her eyes showed true remorse.

Suddenly my appetite vanished, and I felt a little sick. "Sorry. I didn't mean to cause you any emotional trauma."

She jumped from the chair and paced, her tiny kitten heels clacking on the stone. "It's not like I'm going to enjoy summer."

I chose not to offer any words of consolation, which was what she was looking for. In fact, given the fact that I was the one attending the Adventure Program and she would be splashing about for the next six weeks, I didn't have anything to offer. I always feel complete compassion for Jules, as I'm the only one who truly knows the pressure put on her to be perfect at all times, but at that moment I didn't have much sympathy.

She returned to her chair and there might possibly have been the glimmer of tears in her eyes. "I'd trade places with you if I could, Cassidy." She reached for my hands even though they were sticky with grease and juice. "I'll never forget what you did for me. I know it should be me going away to this program too. I know I'm a coward. It kills me that no one knows the truth."

"Well, you could tell everyone what really happened that night. That—"

Her voice rose an octave. "Don't you think I know that? I've tried several times, but I can't."

Honestly? I didn't blame her. Granted, I knew I'd be punished. I just didn't expect my parents to go to such extremes. Even though I'd had plenty of chances to tell, no one would believe me unless Jules backed me up—and I couldn't do it to her anyway. Maybe because it wasn't her fault I left the crime scene at the wrong time. Maybe it was because she's my best friend. Maybe because she always laughs at my jokes even when they aren't funny.

"I've got it!" The spark was back in Jules's face, the tears gone.

"What?"

"Just think about next fall and the football games and the cheerleading."

I snorted and pickle juice came back up through my nose, stinging. "I don't cheer, remember?"

"No, but you could give it a try."

"No thanks."

"Just focus on school and senior year. And then...and then, next fall in school, who knows, maybe this experience and the attention will skyrocket you up the popularity charts. Not that you aren't already popular because everyone loves you." Excitement washed over her in a glow of exuberance, and I couldn't help but feel it too.

"You're forgetting about Ava." Ava Abbot hates my guts ever since I beat her in the spelling bee in the sixth grade. Supposedly, if she'd won, her parents were going to buy her a home theater system for her bedroom. Instead, they bought her a new computer for second place.

Jules waved her delicate hand. "Since when do you care about what Ava thinks?"

"You're right." For the first time, I grabbed Jules hand. "Thanks for the encouragement, but I can handle this summer. Don't worry about me. I'm sure we'll spend afternoons weaving potholders while talking about our issues."

Jules wrapped me in a big hug. She didn't have to say anything. Deep down, I knew she was sorry and felt guilty, but it's hard to stand up to Aunt Lulu.

"Anyway, I wouldn't want to stain your reputation by actually going out for the cheerleading squad."

She laughed. "You might like it once you give a try."

"Joking." Elena and I spent Saturdays making fun of the cheerleaders and their stupid leg kicks and cheers.

She pulled back. "Anyway, you'd never 'stain' my reputation. I'm lucky to have you for a cousin."

A moment hung between us. This was the most honest we'd been in weeks. Since that night. I missed her.

Aunt Lulu's voice floated melodically through the screen door. She was chatting with my mom. Jules put a finger to her lips to shush my chatter so we could listen.

"Well, I'll be more than happy to take Cassandra under my wing this summer as part of her rehabilitation. We must intervene before this ridiculous behavior goes any farther. She might dye her hair or get a lip ring. Heavens!" Her voice lowered so we could barely hear. "She might become promiscuous."

"I am so sorry," Jules whispered, cringing.

"No thanks, Lulu. I can handle my own daughter, but I appreciate the offer."

"Well, if you change your mind at any time, I'm a phone call away. Now it is time for us to leave. Jules! Where are you?" Her voice trilled.

Jules squeezed my hand and left.

I was alone with the sun setting behind the line of trees in my backyard, trying to convince myself that the summer would fly by.

CHAPTER 4

FOR BREAKFAST—MY OFFICIAL Mom-approved one—I ate oatmeal without brown sugar. Not even a spoonful. Nothing but blueberries to counteract the extreme tastelessness. Who invented oatmeal anyway? I bet cardboard would taste better.

For my second breakfast as I drove to the school the next town over, I ate a package of Necco wafers and two peanut butter cups. Did Mom really think I'd stick to this no sugar thing? Because when I'm in a new or unusual situation, I crave sugar. Not only was I attending this Adventure thing, but I had to do it in another school.

I pulled in and sat in my car, trying not to stare at the brick building in front of me, trying not to let my brain imagine death by plastic knives. Maybe I could just sit here all day. Maybe they wouldn't take attendance.

Two seconds later some little car zoomed into the lot and screeched to a stop. I ducked as this total bad boy wanna be—kinda cute too—climbed out of his car. Since I had no desire to do the small talk thing, I watched him strut into the building.

Then I looked at myself in the rearview mirror. "You can do this."

I practically sprinted into the school, because I'd put this off too long. There weren't any signs with arrows pointing me in the right direction, so I wandered and took this time to munch on Skittles.

The guy from the parking lot stepped out of the bathroom. "Are you lost?"

"Nope. Just admiring the great halls of my school's rival."

"Because you're going in the wrong direction. It starts soon, and Mr. Skeeter doesn't like anyone to be late."

I got a closer look at his longish black hair, a bit on the rebellious side, and a lip ring. My first instinct was to ask if I could take him to Aunt Lulu's for Sunday brunch just to see her squirm.

Instead, I made a sound kind of like a hiccup and a gasp. I smiled. "Sorry. I'm kinda nervous."

He regarded me, took in my hair and clothes. "Someone like you would be." Then he strode down the hall.

What? "Excuse me." I ran to catch up. "What do you mean by that?"

He flipped around and stepped real close. I moved back, hitting the lockers. While he studied my eyes, I fell headlong into his greenish-brown ones.

"Just that a girl like you probably doesn't have too many problems. Probably did something stupid one too many times to land here for the summer." A tense moment skittered between us, my heart racing. This was the exact reason I was nervous. That I'd be judged.

He shrugged. "Just saying it like it is. I'm Zeke, by the way." He sniffed my breath. "And don't even think about bringing candy. It's not allowed."

I half-snorted, half-laughed.

"What?"

"Oh, nothing. You wouldn't even begin to understand." I guarantee Mom and Aunt Lulu had something to do with this policy. "And don't use sniffing my breath as an excuse to get close to my lips because these suckers aren't kissing yours." I whirled around in what I hoped was the right direction. Where did that come from? Kissing?

My legs shook as I walked away and then down several hallways. When I neared the only open classroom in the building, I stopped and leaned over, taking deep breaths.

"Are you coming in?" asked a short man with no hair, as in zilcho, entering bowling ball territory. "Or are you going to stand in the hallway?"

"Is this the Adventure Program?"

He nodded with a yawn. "Welcome. Take a seat and wait."

The class was filled with students from every kind of clique. I guess I wasn't alone. Unfortunately, there was only one seat left, next to him. I didn't give him the satisfaction of noting his smirk.

I soon forgot about Zeke as Mr. Boring Pants lectured on about stuff that couldn't hold my attention for longer than five seconds. This summer might be boring, but I'd survive it.

"Time for a backpack check," Mr. Skeeter announced. "Usually do it first thing. Forgot this time."

Everyone got in line. I gripped my backpack, my fingers clenched around the strap, unwilling to cooperate and let go. A warm breeze whispered through from the window, and it brought with it the memories of summer evenings hanging by Jules's pool. As far away as the memories were, the reminder seemed to be her way of encouraging me to at least try. Maybe she was thinking of me right at that moment.

When it was my turn and I held tight, Mr. Skeeter tightened his jaw, waiting. With resignation, I dropped by backpack at his feet.

"If you don't mind I have items of a personal nature in the front pocket." I whispered, "Like tampons."

With a grin, he reached for the front pocket first and slid the zipper open. I thought about collapsing to the ground and faking a seizure, anything to distract him and save myself from anymore humiliation, but before I could do anything he was digging around, then throwing a bag of Skittles on the floor, then my Twix bar, then a small baggie of chocolate chips, then two boxes of Tic Tacs.

I cringed as soft giggles and huffs rippled through the girls in the front row. At the time, in my last moments of desperation, packing this extra stuff seemed like a good idea, items to carry me through the tough times.

"Fine." I huffed. "You found it all. I'm sorry. Okay?"

He flashed me a *Did you think I was stupid?* look. I had hoped...maybe. I then saw my backpack with fresh eyes, the bulging sides and barely closed zippers. I guess I could've been a bit more subtle.

"Hey! Don't I get any privacy?"

I was met with icy cold silence that traveled down my spine and I regretted my last few items. He even went so far as to unzipper the small pocket on the inside where I hid Carter's phone, an extra mp3 player, earbuds, and a pack of gum. After dumping everything out, he tossed the backpack at me.

I sighed and watched as he stuffed all my candy and electronics into a garbage bag he whipped out of the fanny pack around his waist, like every summer there's always that one student who tries to smuggle paraphernalia into the Adventure Program.

This summer that student just happened to be me.

***

AT THE END OF the first week, Mr. Skeeter had the whole group create a circle with our chairs.

He leaned forward, a serious expression on his face as he talked. Guarantee that if Ava or Jules were there they'd already have him convinced to end the program a couple weeks early. They have that kind of influence over people. Influence I obviously don't have.

Mr. Skeeter ran a hand over his bald head as if he missed the days of having hair. "You will all get more out of this program if we learn to trust each other. That starts with sharing a bit of our story." Awkward silence followed. "Anyone willing to be first?"

The tension skyrocketed as a few of the girls seemed to close in on themselves. They ducked behind their hair, they looked off into the corners of the room as if it could curl in on them and hide them, or they stared at the floor.

A shine appeared on his head as if he didn't know what to do if no one talked. "Doesn't mean you have to. We'll have other opportunities, but it's a good time to introduce yourself, tell us a little about your life, and if you're really brave, tell us what brought you here."

Silence lay over us like a thick wool blanket, the kind my dad pulls out when the temperature drops below zero and instead of turning up the heat past 64 degrees he mentions something about the pioneers and survival.

There was the occasional huff and holding of breath—almost as if someone might talk—but then the moment passed. Girls bit their lips or picked at their cuticles, probably hoping this awkward moment would end soon. Boys shoved their hands into their pockets. Zeke played with his lip ring. I sat on my hands and bit my lip for a different reason. I have this problem with silence. It tends to draw the words out of me even when I don't want to talk.

"How about s'mores?" I asked. "Maybe some snacks would make us more comfortable. I don't know about you, but food for me always helps relieve the awkward tension."

Mr. Skeeter turned the glare of disappointment on me and I shut up. Obviously, no one got my joke. I guess that wasn't the kind of sharing he was looking for. Then I caught the expression in his eyes, the caring look he cast on everyone. A horrible feeling sank in my stomach. Here he was, sitting in a stifling classroom with a bunch of troublemakers, and he got me, screwing up his efforts to get us to talk.

"Sorry. Just a suggestion." With a deep sigh I gave up the fight, which is probably how I ended up in the program in the first place. "My name is Cassidy..." That's when my story trailed off. My story of proms and smoke blasters would probably come off sounding pretty stupid.

Zeke leaned forward. In fact, everyone seemed a little more attentive as if curious to listen to my story. "Like I said, my name's Cassidy but don't worry. I didn't rob a bank or anything like that."

I cringed.

"Yes, Cassidy. We're listening." Mr. Skeeter's voice, the way it reverberated, the deep tone, soothing yet familiar, seemed to reach in and encourage me to keep talking. He had a pure talent for this. Maybe someone had recognized this and paid him like a thousand dollars to con kids into sharing the secrets of their heart.

"I guess that's all. I'm Cassidy. I'm not quite ready to share."

"Whatever." The scorn in Zeke's voice was scorching. "The most you could probably tell us is that you drove your daddy's car after you crashed yours."

What? I wanted to march over and slug him one. I drove my mom's van and sometimes the car. I studied him and saw the moment of hesitation as if he knew he went too far.

"Yeah, I guess someone like you would think that," I spit out. I felt like I was back in an elementary cafeteria, defending my tater tots.

Everyone glared at me, like they immediately took Zeke's side. Tension sparked, and Mr. Skeeter jumped in with his soothing voice. "Now, now. This is a safe place for everyone."

Zeke eased back in his chair but not before sending me a scathing look.

Instead of asking anyone else to share, Mr. Skeeter talked a little bit about the next day and his expectations of us over the next six weeks. I tuned him out and kept sneaking evil looks at Zeke, hoping he'd be on the receiving end of one.

Mr. Skeeter coughed, probably to wake everyone from their daydreams. "I think we'll work in pairs starting tomorrow." He turned to Zeke and me. "And you two will have the whole summer to work out your differences. As partners."

Figured.

Week One

Summer was never going to end. Something I never thought I'd ever say or think.

Week Two

This summer was like a piece of Laffy Taffy melting in the sun on top of your phone or stuck on the bottom of your favorite flip-flops—ruined forever.

I was pretty sure my friends were having the worst summer ever. I bet they were bored to death and wondering why it didn't feel the same. Hint: I wasn't there. They just didn't realize it, because if they had they would've sent a homing pigeon with a message, or used a flashlight at night with a Morse cord message or broken in with ski masks to break me out for a night of fun.

CHAPTER 5

"YOU'D BETTER NOT DROP ME," I half-growled, half-threatened.

Zeke flashed me his innocent smile. "What? Don't you trust me, brat?"

"Trust a bad boy with a lip ring? I'm not so sure about that. You boys do have a reputation." We were a few weeks in and just barely on the verge of calling a truce and maybe sorta becoming friends.

He stood with his arms out, and I was supposed to fall backwards and trust he'd catch me. These activities were supposed to increase the chances of our sharing our life stories. Not happening.

Mr. Skeeter peered at us, jotting down notes. "That's the whole point of the exercise. To build trust. Now carry on!"

"That's right," Zeke whispered. "Are you scared?"

"No." I crossed my arms, ready to knock his smug grin into outer space.

He shrugged. "That's okay. We can fake it if you want. I understand the chicken complex."

For about three seconds we stared each other down. "I'm ready," I muttered.

I turned my back to him and closed my eyes. The warm summer breeze whispered through. I listened to the gasps and giggles of all the other partners, and a couple thuds and groans.

"Are you sure?" I peeked behind my shoulder. "Make a muscle for me."

"What?"

"That's right. I want to make sure you can catch me."

He stepped closer. "You want proof?"

"Yes."

"Okay, if that's what you need." In one swoop, Zeke had me over his shoulder and ran across the soccer field. I bounced on his shoulder, which felt like I was riding a camel with a pointy hump. The colors blurred and, even though I wanted to be furious and pound his back, I laughed so hard I couldn't breathe.

"Stop!" I gasped.

"What? I can't hear you!"

After flailing my arms, I grabbed hold of the skin on his arm and started pinching. Finally, he slowed. When he tried to lower me, I fell, and we landed in a pile.

A quiet voice spoke over us. "What is going on here?" It was Mr. Skeeter. "Four laps around the field. Now!"

I pushed up to my feet, stifling any remaining giggles. "Sir, I think I'm allergic to exercise, because I get the same kind of symptoms, especially shortness of breath, like my throat is swelling. Could I walk?"

"Make it six laps!"

On our second lap, Zeke said, "Allergic to exercise?"

"I know, I know." I panted between every third word. "I say dumb things sometimes."

"Sometimes?" He smirked.

"Okay, a lot of the time. I can't help it."

We jogged most of it in silence, and I seriously debated the whole allergy angle. As in maybe I could forge a doctor's note. When we finished the laps, I collapsed under the shade of a tree. "I think I'm going to die."

Zeke leaned against the tree, sweat making his hair kinda stick up. "It was worth it."

"What? Running? I'm not so sure. You could probably put in for a new partner." I didn't even want to think about how beautiful I looked on the verge of passing out and puffing like a train engine.

"No. Getting you to see that maybe I can have fun. That I'm more than just the bad boy."

I pondered his words and how often stereotypes follow us. Okay, so maybe, more than once I'd commented on his lip ring and the whole bad boy image. "Most of the time, I'm just kidding with you about that. Anyway, the bad boy image is probably better than the rich, spoiled brat."

"True." He plucked a piece of grass and chewed on it. His face grew serious. I could practically see the thoughts churning in his mind. "I've tried real hard to fight against that bad boy image." He fell silent for a moment, then said, "I don't want to end up like my parents."

My back prickled. This was starting to sound too much like a friendship and that we didn't hate each other, which I knew was false because he poked fun at me constantly.

"Then don't."

"What?" he asked.

"End up like your parents. Pick out one thing you don't like about them and do the exact opposite every day."

"Huh," then he kinda stared at me like I was Yoda.

"I do it every day."

"Might be easy for you to say with everything handed to you for free."

I stood, tried my best to smooth my hair down, and walked away. I'd never corrected him on my whole spoiled brat stereotype. He'd assumed and I'd let it go. We had spent several weeks together, and he still couldn't see past that?

"Hey, where you going? We're supposed to do some partner thing."

"I'm going to weave some potholders," I called over my shoulder. Even though we both knew that was a complete lie, because they'd forgotten to hire an arts and crafts director.

Guess we weren't meant to be friends after all. Not if he couldn't see past something in me that wasn't even true.

Week Three

It was extremely difficult to focus my thoughts on Michael and a first date and prom when being partnered with someone like Zeke. I deserved a page in the World's Book of Records for the person with the highest tolerance for someone who was annoying and constantly calling me a brat.

Week Four

After a particularly long and mentally exhausting day of exchanging barbs with Zeke, I came home from camp and wrote an email to God, listing all the reasons Zeke shouldn't be accepted into heaven when he arrives at the pearly gates.

Then I included Santa too. Zeke should expect a rather large lump of coal this December.

CHAPTER 6

ALL SUMMER, I'D WORKED on a super-secret, top-priority, no-one-could-see-this-or-I'd-have-to-move-to-Alaska-and-adopt-an-alias list. Every night, I'd flop on my bed, sip my organic green tea—oh, how I longed for the days of soda and cheese curls—and add to my ever growing list of ways to help Michael realize his true feelings for me.

My goal was to write down every conceivable plan and then narrow it down from there.

1. Bring him donuts every morning.

2. Memorize and sing elfin songs from Middle Earth. (Convince Carter to accompany me on the guitar.)

3. Play hard to get. (This one doesn't always work for me.)

4. Make him jealous. (Definitely has potential. Possibly pay someone to take me out on some dates. Make

sure Michael is there. Make sure the guy is at least somewhat cute. Make sure Jules helps with wardrobe.)

5. Break a leg and enlist his help for weeks. (This depends on the Florence Nightingale Effect. Possible problems: the pain factor, what if he doesn't help?)

6. Memorize the Periodic Table of Elements and casually insert into conversation. (This could be too time intensive.)

I broke out of my mad brainstorming session when someone knocked on my bedroom door.

"Go away, Carter."

"It's me. Jules."

In a scramble, I shoved my list inside my notebook and slid it under my pillow. I flipped over on my bed. If possible, Jules's hair had turned three shades lighter and she was tan—in a good way, not in the I'll-have-skin-cancer-kind-of-way. Pfft. Summer fun with friends is highly overrated.

"Do I know you?" I tapped my head. "I'm positive I do. Is it Julia? No, wait. Jemini?"

"You dork."

I laughed with her. "Sorry, it's just been weeks since I've seen anyone."

She plopped down on the bed. "That's why I'm here. The Program is more than halfway over, and we should celebrate. I'm here to connect you with the outer world. Ask me anything."

More like she was still feeling guilty, but I was never one to turn down a celebration. What an opportunity. I wished she'd given me fair warning so I could come up with a good list.

"Did Ava move to Antarctica?" Jules gave me the look. "I'll take that as a no. Has summer been completely boring and a flop and you can't wait for school to start?"

"Definitely," she said with a smile. "Go ahead, ask me about him."

"Who?" I twirled a piece of my hair like I didn't have a clue what she was talking about.

"Michael—your soul mate?"

"Oh, right." I sighed. "How's he doing?" Not that I expected her to know details.

She hesitated, her eyebrows scrunched. "Well, it's been kinda weird. Since you haven't been around, things have shifted. I've actually seen him a couple times. Other than his pointy ears and occasional voice impersonations and random movie trivia, he's not too bad. Or maybe we've all just matured now that it's almost our senior year."

"Huh." That was all I could say, when questions were screaming on the inside. He was moving up the social ladder? What if he'd completely forgotten about me? This required immediate attention. "I'm so glad you stopped by. Are you willing to help me out on a little adventure?"

She bit her lip.

"Come on. You owe me one." I grabbed a bag from my closet. This idea wasn't on the list, but it was a fantastic one. "Wait here."

Five minutes later, I stood outside my bedroom door, still hidden from Jules's view. I made sure the helmet piece was on straight, and I smoothed the black cape. "Are you ready?"

"Cassidy, if this is one of your crazy—"

I leaped into the room, wielding a Jedi light-up sword thing and sliced at the air with it. "I'm here with a message from the galaxy." I used my best Darth Vader voice, which wasn't very good. "You should take Cassidy out on a date." Then I pulled my best life-threatening fight moves meant to instill fear in the hearts of all. Or at least enough mild panic that he'd follow through. "Then ask her to prom."

Jules squealed and burst out laughing. Finally, I pulled the helmet off because I couldn't breathe very well and felt slightly claustrophobic and tucked it under my arm. "Should I suggest he takes me out on a date—or go right to prom?"

"Good one. Except I'm here to make you laugh, not the other way around." She rolled off the bed. "Get that ridiculous thing off and we'll go pop the frozen pizza in the oven and watch a marathon of romantic comedies."

"Right. Of course, I was totally kidding." Before I left the room, I added one more to my list.

8. Dress as Darth Vader with a message from the galaxy. With my awesome fight moves, convince him to ask me on a date. (Consider switching that to prom!)

***

EVERY DAY WAS FILLED with team building activities. We all had to crisscross our arms and hold hands and then without letting go, unravel the human knot. All fun and games unless you were holding sweaty palms—not Zeke's.

I lost myself in the day-to-day routine. Every afternoon we had quiet time to journal. I desperately wished for my candy stash in those moments. One day, on our lunch break, I found a spot in the shade and pulled out *War and Peace*, hoping to finish it and impress my teachers this fall.

Zeke plopped down next to me and stretched out his lanky legs. Since our little fight where I hadn't explained why I was angry, we'd only talked in short sentences and spent time together because we had to as partners. Several times, I'd tried to explain that I wasn't the rich brat he took me to be, but each time, the words caught in my throat. Why would he believe me?

"Heavy reading," he said.

"No kidding. It weighs like twenty pounds. You try hauling it around everywhere."

He flashed me a smile as if to say *Lame joke but I'll smile to make you feel better*. The smile faded and he grew serious. "Sorry about the other day and sorry about that first sharing day and everything else. I didn't mean to come down so hard on you."

"No problem." I couldn't help but stare at his smile. I had noticed some time in week three or week four that his bottom teeth were crooked in the most adorable way.

I struggled to pay attention to the tiny words on the page. They blurred in front of me. I closed it with a huff and bit into my brussel sprout and tuna sandwich on organic gluten-free bread. This was the perfect time to tell him everything about prom and smoke blasters and my family's financial status.

He fiddled with his lip ring. "For the record, I think you're brave."

"Thank you." Keeping it short and sweet was the way to stay away from word vomit. "Um, for what?" Reading *War and Peace?*

"It's hard to be the first to share, even if you weren't able to go into details."

I swung my legs around and stared him in the eyes. "You should understand a little bit about that." So much for short and sweet, but I'd wanted to bring this up since that first day.

"How's that?"

"You haven't exactly shared too much about your life."

Something flicked off in his eyes like he was trying not to remember. His slender hands twisted together and he was the one staring at *War and Peace*.

"Sorry about that. You don't have to share anything with me." Would I ever just shut up? That's how I got into the whole mess in the first place.

He untwisted his hands and stared off. "My dad's in jail. My mom took off. I live with my uncle, who moves around because of his job. I've been to a different school every year. This coming year is no different. I'll be spending my senior year, again, as the new student. A stranger. It takes a few months just to have a decent conversation with someone. End of story."

"Sorry," I whispered. In comparison, I could never share my story. It would just confirm his initial thoughts on my bratty background. Even if my family wasn't rolling in green dough, we were still together.

"So really, why are you here?" He focused on me.

"I got in trouble." There was something ironic about half-truths. Almost like adding both butterscotch and hot fudge sauce to ice cream at the same time. And at this point, we were kinda friends. "I like to be a woman of mystery."

He looked away and played with his lip ring.

I felt stupid for not telling the truth after he opened up. "It's not that I don't trust you or anything, obviously we've done enough trust exercises to be past that point but..."

"But what?"

"Well, I, er, you know..."

How would he possibly understand my life of proms and pranks when his dad was in jail? My story would look like a mockery with me the rich, spoiled brat he pegged me to be.

"You know what?" He stood and brushed off his jeans. "I've been trying all week, but it takes two in a friendship, and I'm clearly alone in this one."

Week Five

Mr. Skeeter pulled Zeke and I aside and quietly mentioned that if we couldn't figure out a way to get along then he'd assign extra partner assignments.

Week Six

Yay! This was almost over! I'd never have to see Zeke again. Friends! Parties! Here I come.

CHAPTER 7

IT WAS THE LAST day of the Adventure Program. After lunch, Mr. Skeeter led a special meeting. "Circle up!"

Those had become famous words that I never wanted to hear again. He wanted us to spend the afternoon alone, thinking, and writing in our journal. Hopefully we'd find peace with ourselves and experience that transformative moment when all the answers came together in one final glorious moment, as if heaven opened up and the Lord himself visited.

Somehow, I doubted I'd have some kind of hallelujah moment.

I hunkered down behind the school about ten yards from the woods. The silent landscape stretched out before me, the wild flowers in scattered bunches, the bramble of bushes, and the trees cropping up.

I thought about one thing. When this was over, I needed to kick things into high gear with Michael. I had one year and only one prom left. Obviously, my accidental meet-ups with him over the past year hadn't worked. All the times I wrote my name as Mrs. Michael Greenwood in pretty cursive or carved our initials into tree trunks encircled by a heart or daydreamed about our wedding had done nothing to actually further our relationship.

I was so lost in trying to find my focus that I didn't hear Zeke sneak up behind me until he plopped down. He crossed his arms over his knees, focusing on the wild flowers I'd noticed moments before. "Hey."

I glanced sideways. "So we're talking now?"

"I'd hate to leave our budding friendship on such a bad note. I'm really not a bad guy."

I smiled. "Sometimes we're all misunderstood." I wanted to tell him the truth so bad, but he'd probably scoff and think even less of me.

He let out a soft sigh that I don't think he meant for me to hear, like everything was my fault.

Maybe if I opened up about something personal that would fix everything. "Can I ask you a question?"

He perked up, hope lighting his eyes. "Anything."

"I just want you to know hard this is for me—to ask anyone for help therefore admitting my own weakness." I took a sip of water.

"Go ahead. I'm listening."

"I have somewhat of a personal question to ask."

"I'll try to answer if I can."

"You're a guy..."

"That's what I'm told."

"I wondered if you could share some of the guy point of view with me."

"Um, I guess."

"You should see this one girl work it at my school." I decided not to mention certain names like Ava Abbot in an effort to be gracious. And Karma. "She flips her hair, sticks out her total boob job and bats her eyes like she's got a fake eyelash blocking her vision. She's mean and shallow."

"I've seen my share of those girls. What's your point?"

"Well...do you have any pointers?"

"On what?" His look of peace faded into one of extreme disappointment.

"On how to snag a boy without all those fake things." I kept talking, the words shooting out like leaves in a windstorm, swirling around him, making it worse. "I mean what can a nice, ordinary girl like me do to get the attention, of well, a boy like you?" I realized my mistake. "Not that I want to snag you because I don't. I already know who I'm going to marry, so this isn't even for me...but for a friend who feels like she's a bit too plain Jane to get the boy she knows she's destined to be with and he barely notices her."

Silence settled between us, sharp and fast. Zeke's lips formed into a line, almost disappearing into his mouth.

He took several deep breaths, in and out, before he managed to say anything at all to me.

He spoke, his words soft but packing a punch. "I should've known the first day you were trouble. You might not care, but I do. All this time, you haven't shared one thing about yourself that is deeper than the layer of nail polish chipping on your fingernails."

Ouch. But he didn't stop there.

"You've been one of the hardest people to get to know. I've tried. Everything's a joke for you or a chance to ramble on about bits and pieces of your life that mean nothing to anyone else. I've worked hard to change my life around, to turn out different than my dad."

I straightened up. "That means you failed as a friend because you obviously didn't get to know me very well." *Or I didn't let him in,* a tiny voice said in my head.

He pushed his face into mine and I couldn't help but notice his flawless skin tone. The pores on his nose were practically invisible. "You don't have me fooled one bit. You have a world of hurt and mistrust buried inside that you like to cover up with a bunch of meaningless babble instead of talking about the real stuff. I don't know what or who it is that hurt you but I hope someday you figure it out so you can move forward with your life. I wish you the best. I really do. Just far away from me."

For a brief second I wanted to break down and cry, but anger flared to the surface, burning bright and true. "Thank you for caring so much for my emotional well-being.

I can't wait to tell my parents and friends about the wonderful guy I met here." I had to stop and take in a cleansing breath before I said something I'd regret.

He stood and brushed the dirt off his pants. He started to walk away but stopped to hammer the final nails in the proverbial coffin. "And about snagging a guy like me? You can forget it. Even if a guy's good looking doesn't mean he doesn't have a heart or doesn't want a nice girl. But I wouldn't put you in that category, so go ahead and flip your hair and bat your eyes because that might be your best shot."

"Well, fine then." *Good comeback, Cassidy.*

"Have a nice life." Then he walked away.

His words pierced my heart. That wasn't me. I hadn't been trying to be like Ava, so I couldn't believe he equated me to the likes of her.

So much for using this time to plan and think about my life. At this moment, I didn't have much heart to figure it out anyway.

CHAPTER 8

AHHH. THE SWEET FEELING of waking up on my own, without the blaring sound of my alarm clock. No Adventure Program! Yay!!! And? My grounding was over—everything crucial to life like the Internet, my phone, YouTube, and seeing my friends.

I should be running over to Jules's or maybe Elena's to catch a few minutes with a friend. I should be running downstairs to embrace my parents in a huge hug and tell them how grateful I was for the experience and that it was their best decision ever in the history of their parenting. But I had one prerogative. Michael. He'd be glad to see me.

Leaving the Darth Vader helmet in my closet—worst idea ever—I went downstairs and breezed through the doorway. "Hi, Mom!" I said it extra loud and chipper.

"Cassidy?" Mom whirled around and opened her arms. "Come here."

My feet were rooted to the ground even though I wanted nothing more than to feel her hug. She made up the ground and pulled me into her arms. For a brief second I laid my head on her shoulder like I was a little girl who'd scraped her knee. I squeezed my eyes shut, fighting off the tears. I refused to cry.

"It's finally over, honey. You were such a trooper."

I broke away, my voice cracking at first but I quickly hid that with a cough. "Thanks."

She smiled, her eyes finding mine, her love for me shining through. "What are you going to do today? Sure you won't be bored?"

I plastered on a smile. "I'm going to head out for some ice cream."

My hand was on the doorknob before my mom responded. "Remember, no sugar."

"No problem. I didn't really want ice cream anyway, or cake. I mean the frosting will just rot all my teeth and what with school coming all our extra money needs to go to clothes and food and what about the mortgage. Heavens! Wouldn't want to fall behind in that area..." *Shut up, Cassidy!* I took a deep breath. "I'll be home later."

I didn't stick around to see the look on Mom's face. I borrowed the van and drove to Ye Olde Ice Cream Shoppe. I ordered from the outside window and found a spot at one of the tables. I was almost done with my hot fudge sundae when my friends exited from a blue two-door car.

Michael climbed out of the front seat, followed by Elena. Out of the back tumbled Jules, Ava, and Jasper. I froze, unable to move, unable to think. Elena spotted me first, and I debated running away.

She was the first to reach me. "Hey, girl. Your grounding over?"

I wanted to act as normal as possible. "Today. Just like I said six weeks ago at the start of summer. But I know how summer gets with time slipping by faster than a roller coaster." I waved my hand and forced a laugh. "It's so hard to keep track of everything. Never mind who's coming or going." *Or when your friend has been set free from prison.*

Elena pulled back, her face paling a bit under the suntan she most likely acquired from the hours spent lazing in her backyard without me. I knew that would happen but seeing the result of my absence and how smoothly their lives had continued and changed, prickled under my skin. An uncomfortable feeling, and I'd never felt that way with my friends.

I tilted my head and pasted on my best smile. "How about drinks? Soda? Iced-tea? On me."

"Really?" Michael perked up. He'd barely sent me a glance but the mention of free food got his attention.

I had hoped my subliminal message would steer them toward ordering drinks, but Michael and Elena ordered sandwiches and fries. Jules and her gang asked for cones. "Great. I'll be right back."

I strode through the doors, mumbling their orders over and over again. It couldn't be too hard to mess up a sandwich and fries for Elena, and a burger with no pickle—or was that extra pickles—for Michael. The cones I could remember. I arrived at the register and placed the order, going with extra pickles on the side.

I pulled out my change purse and opened it to find nothing but a couple dimes. I could've sworn I had more than that. I must've spent the last of my money on my ice cream. The girl behind the counter looked at me, her eyes blinking, waiting for me to fork over the cash or a card.

"Well, you see, I'm an old-timer here, by the way I'm Cassidy. I know customers aren't allowed to rack up a credit but I was wondering..." I ran out of words and the last breath seeped out.

With a roll of her shoulders, the girl said, "You don't have any money?"

"Not really, but I could come back later and pay. I'm having a welcoming home party with my friends and I thought I had more cash on me. I can go home and round up the change and come back and pay."

I bit my lip, holding my breath, already knowing the answer before she said it. "Sorry. Credit isn't allowed." Her eyes shifted to the next person in line.

My whole body sagged. I glanced out the front windows at my friends already laughing and at ease, now that I was out of the picture. Or that was what it felt like. I squared my shoulders. I'd never run and I wouldn't start. "Five ice waters then."

"Um, that'll be twenty-five cents per cup."

"Seriously?"

She nodded.

"No thanks." I turned and shuffled across the tiled floor. I didn't want the front door to come but eventually I was there, my hand on the knob. I turned it and the breeze drifted through. The door clanged shut behind me. My friends didn't even notice until I pulled up a chair next to them.

For some reason, I couldn't look at Michael. After all our nights talking at his window and acting out movie scenes, I shouldn't feel tongue-tied, but he wasn't usually in our group, which made everything awkward.

"Precious, my precious," he said in his creepy Gollum voice.

Everyone echoed it back and then cracked up laughing. It hurt deep down inside because that was my thing with Michael. I hated every minute of it but acted out those stupid scenes and pretended to be Gollum for him, for us, for our future.

His chair scraped across the cement of the patio. "I'll be right back. Bathroom."

"So, tell us everything," Jules asked hesitantly like she wanted to know but didn't want to know.

Elena laughed, but it did nothing to cheer me or replace the emptiness. She leaned closer, dimples flashing, her blonde hair swinging forward. "I want to know about the guys. Meet any cute bad boys?"

An image of Zeke flashed in my head, his longish dark hair, his smirky smile, lip ring, and his crooked teeth. I squashed that image before my blood started boiling and I had to run ten miles to deal with my anger. I laughed instead. "Of course. Total hotties!"

I couldn't seem to stop thinking about Zeke and what a pain in the royal butt he was, and that was when I figured out how to take my revenge on him. Even though he'd never even want to walk down the street with me, never mind a real date, I could force him into all sorts of romance with me, without him knowing, and make my summer sound not so miserable.

I placed my chin on my hands and stared off dreamily, as girls will do when they've found true love. I let out a dramatic sigh. "There was this one guy. So hot." I fanned my face. "It was love at first sight over group activities and trust falls."

"Really?" Elena looked doubtful.

I recovered. "Of course, there wasn't a lot of time for romance but we found ways to connect here and there. I think if we were to meet under any other circumstances, I probably wouldn't have even noticed him."

"He was hot and you wouldn't have noticed him? What if he were to show up at school? You wouldn't notice a cute guy?"

"Of course. I just can't say that he's the kind of guy I usually like."

Elena relaxed. "Did you kiss?"

"Oh boy, did we ever." Jules watched me, her eyes knowing and questioning. Like she didn't believe me. "The first kiss was the most romantic thing ever. We snuck out and he led me to the middle of the soccer field." I sighed again. "Pure romance."

The door closed and I heard the footsteps. I knew before he sat down that it was Michael, and all my feelings and plans rushed back. I couldn't let him think I'd betrayed our love. He'd never see or admit his true feelings.

"The rest gets too intimate. I'll tell you later." I expertly changed the subject. "So Michael, anything exciting happen this summer?"

His face turned slightly pink. "Just the normal." He tapped his watch. "Maybe I should check on our food."

Michael couldn't check on the food. There was no food! I jumped up. "I'll go. I'm not used to sitting around doing nothing anyway."

I stepped inside the door and leaned against the frame. A hot prickly feeling came over me, and I had to practice my breathing technique. I'd have to tell them our orders got messed up and it would be another hour so we should go for pizza instead. That would work. Everyone loves pizza as much as ice cream and fries.

I peeked back outside. I couldn't stand Ava, who always treated me like a queen would a peasant, and

Jasper? Ugh. He swaggered around school, muscles flexing, pearly whites flashing. All the girls swooned, even I did a little bit. Some things can't be helped, like biology. Now I had to get rid of all of them. If I ran, my entire social structure would collapse.

After a deep breath, and quickly debating stealing trays of food from the counter, I decided to face the music, but Jules entered just as I was about to exit.

She touched my arm. "Is everything okay?"

"Well, um..." I couldn't lie to her. "I thought I had more money but I couldn't even pay for the cups for ice water."

She laughed. "Come on. I left my purse at home, but I'll explain it to them."

Back at the table, Ava barely acknowledged me. I think Jasper had fallen in love with his muscles as he continued to flex.

Jules put on her annoyed face. "Guys, it's way too backed up in there. I took back our order. I'm more in the mood for pizza anyway."

Jasper smiled, cocky and sure. He hung his arms around Ava and Jules like they were his harem. "No. Let's head to my place, girls. Everyone's welcome."

They all flashed gooey smiles up at him, like he wore a cape and could fly. I wanted to puke. They turned, laughing, not giving us another thought, and headed back to the car. Elena followed.

Michael gathered his stuff, mumbling about pizza, and trotted after Elena like a puppy. I told them I'd be sure to catch up with them later even though I had absolutely no intention of doing so. When they drove away, I slumped into a chair.

An empty feeling grew and swirled, reminding me that they didn't throw a party, they didn't mark their calendars, and Michael didn't miss me enough to hug me...or he forgot about his true feelings for me. I mean would a tap on the shoulder have killed him?

Freedom was nothing like I'd imagined.

***

BACK AT HOME, I shut myself up in my bedroom with my goldfish and stayed there the rest of the day and night. I came out for breakfast the next morning then went back to my cave.

The Taylor Swift strumming stopped next door and then I heard a knock. The door opened, slightly creaking, then Carter flopped on my bed next to me.

"Are you okay?"

"Sure."

"Mom and Dad are worried."

"Pfft. I'm fine." I rolled onto my back. "How's Taylor Swift working out for you?" He coughed like he didn't want to tell me. "Tell me. Maybe I can offer some sympathy."

"Actually, I uploaded a YouTube video of me playing the guitar and singing Love Story and I've gotten a thousand more friends on Facebook and ten girls from school have called for dates."

Honestly? I was flabbergasted. Guys playing Taylor Swift and snagging hot dates would only work in the life of my brother. "How do you do it?"

He hesitated, probably sensing my sinking discouragement. "I just put myself out there. Sometimes you have to take chances." He nudged me. "That's my secret. You only hear about the times my efforts succeed. I'm good at hiding the failures."

I laughed. "Your failures still probably end up with you on a date."

"True. But it's still a failure in comparison." He stood. "Your time will come. Just take a chance."

"Cassidy?" Mom called from downstairs. "Elena's coming up."

Carter vanished from my room and I snagged a book so it looked like I wasn't a total loser. She appeared in the doorway and lightly knocked. "Can I come in?"

"Of course. Why are you even asking?"

"You seemed off yesterday. I wasn't sure if you'd want to see me."

"That's dumb. Of course, I want to see you."

She took Carter's place on the bed. "You never caught up with us like you promised."

"Still needed sleep. I felt like a zombie." Maybe that was the truth. Maybe if I could sleep for twenty-four hours and get a memory wipe of Zeke's smirk, I could feel like myself again.

She lay on the bed next to me. "Tell me more about this guy."

The only reason Elena completely believed me was because she didn't know about Michael. If she did, she'd know I'd never betray him like that.

I launched into a full spiel, wishing Zeke could listen and squirm. "It was heavenly. He was hot like a cocky jerk but softer because we had so many afternoons just talking when we were supposed to be doing trust activities."

"So I guess it wasn't all that bad. You probably had more fun than we did here."

"Definitely." I blinked back the tears and fought the growing ache in my throat. "It was like one big party. I didn't want it to end."

"Oh."

There's always a moment where you wish you could push rewind and take back a moment or a word spoken and start fresh. This was one of those times, but I couldn't see past those few seconds where I desperately needed to redeem my miserable summer in the eyes of one of my friends.

"Ready for the start of school?" she asked, but any enthusiasm was gone and the life seeped out of our conversation.

"I guess."

Her voice grew wistful. "Our senior year. Everything we've been looking forward to for years. The Christmas dance, the yearbook snapshots, prom..."

"No kidding. It's going to be a blast."

We managed a few more completely awkward comments and then she mumbled something about organizing stuff for school, which had to be a complete lie because Elena is the most organized person I know, so her pencils were all in a line after the last day of junior year.

She stood and said goodbye. I grasped at what to say, how to bring back the honesty we always had, but it slipped away the closer she got to the door. Then she was gone.

That night, I made a declaration of sorts. I would gain back everything I'd lost. Somehow or another, I'd redeem myself, and I'd achieve my goal of attending senior prom with Michael.

CHAPTER 9

YUP. THE FIRST DAY of my senior year was the worst. It all started with Carter dashing into the shower before me, his bathrobe flapping in the breeze. Since when does that happen? Never! Then he took an extra long time in the shower and winked at me as he swaggered back to his room, like he used up all the hot water as some sort of revenge.

"I love cold showers, so there."

I had bigger problems, much bigger, like boys, and I didn't have any easy answers. Showered and ready for school, I rushed through the kitchen, grabbing a piece of toast with peanut butter, but Mom hovered, fidgeting, trying to say something.

"Out with it." I crunched into the toast, enjoying a stress-free moment of melting peanut butter. "If you don't tell me now, I'll have this lecture of doom hanging over my head all day, and that could affect the start of my relationship with teachers who ultimately hold my collegiate future in their hands."

She sighed. "Oh, Cassidy. Do you need to be so dramatic?"

"Yup. Now tell me."

"We feel really bad about this past summer and that it was before your senior year and you didn't see your friends much and—"

"Mom." My tone said it all: get on with it.

"Oh, right." She smoothed her shirt and fiddled with the dirty dishes on the counter. That's when I knew how bad this really was, except I couldn't pretend to barf in the bathroom or I'd be late for school. "Your father and I feel it might help for you to talk to someone about this past summer and...last spring. I know you pretend that all is just fine and dandy, but we see past that."

I sagged against the counter, completely deflated, but she wasn't done.

"As your parents, we see the haunted, empty look on your face when you don't think anyone's looking."

"What?" I guess I needed more make-up.

"We see past your jokes and long speeches. We thought it might be good for you to participate in a peer support group that the Program recommends. Talking to others about everything might resolve any underlying emotional trauma."

"Wow. Someone's been reading up on their psychology."

Mom pulled me into a hug before I could pull back. She squeezed me tight and all her compassion, love, and caring oozed into me; and for a second, I felt safe and loved and like everything would be okay. I'm sure that was part of her evil plan.

"Fine. If it'll make you and Dad feel better."

***

THE DOORS TO HIGH SCHOOL swung open and I walked through, breathing in the excitement of a new year, of a senior year, filled with promises of laughter, bonding, good times. The kind that stay with you forever.

The further I went into the building, the more I noticed the whispers and the sideways glances. That should be expected. After all, I was *that* girl. The one who smoked out senior prom, the one who got in trouble with the cops, the one who went to some day camp for kids that were about to be kicked out of school.

Elena appeared at my side as I headed to first period. She tossed her pixie cut from her face. Her faux diamond earrings sparkled, and she looked so put together. Even with all my plans and dreams for change, I couldn't pull that off.

She chatted about some mysterious new guy, even though Michael straggled along a few feet behind us, hanging on her every word. I tried to ignore the sick feeling in the pit of my stomach at his clearly misguided puppy love/infatuation. I'd have to work hard to recover the ground I'd lost over the summer.

I slumped into first period English with a figurative cloud hanging over my head. I managed all morning, barely, ignoring the whispers and outright comments directed toward me. I had to bite my lip or the truth would come exploding out, because I was tired of being the only one taking the blame. A simple pact had snowballed into something I never asked for and never wanted.

The worst moment—or second worst moment— happened at lunchtime. I stood outside the glass windows and peeked inside the cafeteria, searching for my friends. First, I found Michael and an immediate blush rose in my face, whether from anger or humiliation I wasn't sure. I squelched the tiny pitter-patter of my heart. He strode across the cafeteria, pushed past several girls until he was walking with Elena. He followed her to a table and then sat next to her. Even though Elena chatted with everyone but him, he seemed not to notice.

My feet were rooted to the tiled floor, and I barely noticed the lunch crowds rushing into the cafeteria. I flipped around and headed to the next best lunch spot, saved for when one has been humiliated: outside the side door by the science wing. I could eat in peace without ending up with digestive problems.

As I nibbled on my chicken salad sandwich, the reality of my life crashed through. I wanted to change but didn't know how, and someone had poked Michael with Cupid's arrow except he was falling for the wrong girl. I leaned against the brick wall and raised my face to God above. "Holy heck, what am I going to do?"

I stumbled through classes, hiding my flushed face because hot prickles kept invading my body every time I caught sight of Michael flirting with Elena. I barely answered any questions and hid out in the bathroom as much as possible to avoid anyone and everyone.

At the end of the day, with dread still hovering, I knocked on the guidance counselor's door. They supervised this peer support group Mom suggested for me.

"Come on in."

I pictured Mr. Grabowski sitting behind his desk, probably reading dirty magazines in his spare time. He'd been a guidance counselor for over thirty five years. Most kids knew he should've retired like ten years ago.

I pushed inside, the words spilling out my mouth. "I really don't think this is needed. I mean six weeks at that day camp is like a life time's worth of counseling, don't you—"

Mr. Grabowski nodded to the chairs in front of his desk.

Zeke leaned back in a chair, with a smirk, though he quickly masked it and smiled warmly. I took in his messed-up hair as if his first day at a new school didn't go so well.

Warmth radiated from him toward me that didn't make any sense considering how we left things.

"You!"

"Hi, Cassidy."

"What are you doing here?" The hot prickles rushed over me again, a feeling that I was in trouble and about to be found out. I imagined everyone finding out Zeke was my lover boy and that he'd eventually hear that rumor.

"What a surprise, huh?" The smile reached his greenish-brown eyes and he flipped his hair back in a way that would make most girls swoon.

I sat in one of those chairs, just cushy enough to make someone feel comfortable, so kids will spill their innermost, darkest secrets. Of course, every other room in the school gets plastic chairs. What a rip off. I felt numb, completely locked on the inside and for the first time in my life I didn't have anything to say. Or, I did, but at first I was in too much shock.

Mr. Grabowski cleared his throat and launched into a speech, which I'm surprised he didn't have notecards for it was so classic and manipulative. "Welcome to the first of many peer support groups following your experience at The Adventure Program." He droned, lecturing that we'd get out of this what we put in and what a great opportunity this year presented. A chance to start over and make better decisions. Just as I was about to nod off, he wound down and ended with, "Let's try to get through this year without too much drama. How does that sound?"

I nodded, trying not to peek at Zeke.

Mr. Grabowski said a bunch of other stuff that I completely ignored. After about fifteen minutes, he glanced at his watch. "Each session, I'll be in the connected office with the door open so you both can feel free to talk. I'll be available if you need me."

With that, he grabbed his briefcase, laid out our counseling times for the next few months, and then left. Zeke was the first to speak.

"I was a total jerk the last day of camp. As I've been told, I was feeling the stress and took it out on you."

"Sure, no problem." A part of me felt relieved that we wouldn't have to spend hours rehashing that last day. That fight was the least of my problems.

Sweat broke out as my pulse increased. I mean, Zeke was at my school! He'd meet my friends and I'd see him every day. If everyone figured out I'd outright lied about my incredible romance with him, it would be disastrous on so many levels.

He broke into my thoughts. "Yeah, but I was still a jerk. Maybe we can be friends?"

I considered his words, and I didn't fully understand his intention or the sudden flip in his attitude toward me. This friendship just couldn't happen, even if a part of me wanted it. I shot up from chair, almost knocking it over.

"Gosh, you don't want to be friends with me. I'm not like other girls and who knows maybe that's my problem? I don't fit the mold. I never have. I see life differently. From a perspective that's all my own." I backed up toward the door, catching my breath. "You'd be much better off making other friends." What I didn't say was that I didn't really believe his apology. He obviously couldn't stand me, so I had no idea why he was pretending to want to be my friend.

"I told you. I'm sorry." His voice sounded hard, like his emotions were walking a line too. "Anyway, I like all that about you."

I laughed out loud. "You don't have to pretend to like me to clear your conscience. I forgive you, okay? Now you can sleep again at night." At the door, I turned. "And as far as you and me, no one will know we met at the Adventure Program." I thought about the lies I'd let him believe about me. He thought I was rich. He thought I was a cheerleader. "I have to go to cheer practice." Then I slammed the door.

I guess I was going to try out for cheerleading.

I whirled around only to crash into another student. Of course, the way my day was going it was no surprise that it was Michael. His books crashed to the floor, and he spluttered an apology. Then he saw me.

I stared at him, hard and convincing. "Don't worry. I'm not stalking you. And for the record, you crashed into me."

I stormed off to become the best cheerleader this school had ever seen.

CHAPTER 10

I'M SURE CHEERLEADING IS a complicated sport, an art in and of itself, not something to be taken lightly. Jules takes cheerleading as seriously as Carter takes dating girls.

The best way to approach a delicate matter like convincing my cousin to use her influence with the coach to get me on the squad was to observe first and then come up with a plan of attack. I crawled under the bleachers, under the stringy cobwebs and among the littered trash, and peered between the seats.

The first time a girl was thrown up in the air with a straddle-jump-leap-thing where her legs went higher than her hips, I felt woozy. Spots appeared, and I had to crouch and get my breathing under control. The last thing I wanted to do was pass out under the bleachers, knock myself out on a rock and not be found for days.

I was not made for anything that contorted the body into strange positions. When we were younger, every time Carter and I played Twister, I lost big time. Carter should be the one trying out for cheerleading—it could be his upgraded method of getting girls. No doubt it would work for him.

I stood, daring to peek out again. All I saw were flips and jumps and straight, jerky movements. But at a closer look it was the same girls being thrown and doing the flip things. Some stayed on the fringes just doing the cheers. That could be me.

Sucking it up and reminding myself of all that was at stake—like my reputation—I strolled out onto the field and stood close to Jules. She didn't notice me at first, but some of the girls did, like Ava, and they nodded to Jules. When she turned and saw me, the look on her face told me everything. She strode over.

She tried to smile. "I'm in the middle of practice."

"I'd like to try out for cheering."

She grabbed my arm and gently led me away from the girls. "Tryouts were two weeks before school started. We have our team."

I don't know what came over me. Maybe a day of seeing Michael drool all over Elena had pushed me over the edge. Maybe it was because Zeke was at the school and I had the sudden compulsion to cheer. I figured this one small favor was nothing compared to the huge favor I'd done for her last spring, and I'd pay the consequences for that probably forever. I'd lost Michael. Elena and I were walking on a tightrope. One wrong move and I'd fall into the abyss called Loserville, where I had no friends and I'd permanently eat lunch outside, even in the winter.

I took a deep breath, mustering all the courage I had. "You're the one who always encourages me to step up and try to fit in. You're the one who said last summer you were willing to pay back the favor. Well, this is a first step. I know it's a lot to ask."

"This is about prom somehow?" She crossed her arms across her chest.

I squirmed. "Prom is just a small part. I also want to change. Meet new people."

She sighed, glancing back at her friends, her face paler than usual. "I'm more than happy to help, you know that, but don't you think this is going a little too far?"

"It's my last chance. It's our senior year."

We were in a draw, staring at each other, a lifetime of memories flashing between us. All the times we hung out at family events. All the times we were more like best friends.

"I can't make the final decision, and Coach isn't here." She sighed. "Practice with us today, and I'll talk to Coach for you."

***

I KNOCKED ON THE door of the guidance room two days later. After a long and enlightening conversation with my parents I came to one conclusion. I didn't have a choice but to sit through these sessions, but I didn't have to like it and I didn't have to cooperate.

"Come on in."

I waltzed in and sat down, a stone-cold maiden from a fantasy novel who would keep all her secrets under a layer of ice. I stared ahead, trying to ignore the dark, mysterious eyes next to me, pulling me in. Never mind the snug-fitting black T-shirt.

Mr. Grabowski got started right away, lecturing long and hard about responsibility in this day and age. I was almost falling asleep and out of my chair, when he stood. "Time for you two to talk." He gathered his papers. "I'll be in the other room."

After he left, we sat in silence.

This time I broke it. I couldn't help but ask one tiny question. Harmless really. "So all the girls falling over themselves to get to know the new guy? The mysterious bad boy?"

He chuckled and did the hair flip thing. "Is that what they're saying?"

I snorted. "Like you don't know."

He shrugged. "Not really. I don't care about those kinds of things." He shifted in his chair and redirected the conversation at the same time. "How has school been for you?"

"Fine." Who was I kidding? Totally stunk so far. In the past two days, I'd gone out for a sport I hate, and the guy I was totally in love with was in love with my friend.

Zeke leaned forward, his greenish-brown eyes focused on me. "I don't buy for one second that a million different thoughts aren't whirling through your head right now."

"Don't think you know me just because you spent six weeks with me."

"You'd be amazed at everything I figured out about you during all those trust activities. You were like an open book." He lowered his voice. "By week three we were all pretty vulnerable."

"Why don't you tell me about you then, Mr. Vulnerable?"

His eyes flickered over me, questioning. "I'd rather focus on you."

"No thanks." Even though my stomach did this strange flutter thing. "I really have nothing to share."

"How's cheering going for you?" He smirked like he knew my secret, but he couldn't, could he?

"I love cheering. It's fantastic. Live for it."

He nodded. "Yeah, I bet. Seems to fit the profile of the snooty rich girl who has to suffer from having so much money."

I ignored him the rest of the time, tapping my fingers against the arm of the chair. Each tense second felt like an eternity until our session was over, and then I booked it out of there.

***

I HATED EVERY MINUTE of cheerleading. The Coach agreed to give me a trial period, but only because Jules was captain, and a girl had dropped out before school had started. The next two weeks were pure torture. Jules acknowledged my presence but was so focused on the team that she had no time for hand-holding.

I'll be honest: I was a terrible cheerleader and I hadn't been this sore in forever. I hobbled through the halls while trying to explain why I'd put myself through this to Elena.

"Since when did you become a cheerleader?" Elena cast me a questioning look. "Is this another side effect of your summer experience?"

All I wanted to do was break down and sob and spill the truth about everything. "I'm just trying new things, experimenting. Trying to be a more well-rounded person."

Elena snorted. "Have fun with that."

After that conversation it wasn't brought up again. She tolerated me because we'd been friends forever. Sitting in the cafeteria and hearing the laughter and the chatter, in the midst of a sea of students, just like me, made me feel alone. Like a wall divided me from everyone and everything I knew.

Zeke followed through and acted like he didn't know me. He seemed to buy that I was a cheerleader, but I wondered if it was all worth it.

It was after a particular miserable cheering experience where I blanked out on the cheer and stumbled through it, copying the movements, but always a step behind that I sank into an oblivion of depression. That night after dinner, when my parents settled into their reading and murmured conversations—probably about me—I sneaked outside. My feet remembered the path and I stopped at the edge of Michael's yard.

There'd be no stargazing or excited whispered conversations through the window or re-enactments. I sank down against a tree, watching and staring at the darkened room where Michael spent most of his time. We'd spent many evenings together—or had it just seemed like a lot to me? I remembered every look, expression, and twitch of his lips. Had I imagined his feelings? I couldn't have, but I think he liked to pretend they never existed after I got in trouble with the cops.

I had hours invested in Michael. All the nights I'd spent daydreaming, all the conversations I had with my goldfish, and all the planning that went into our meet-ups. A part of me didn't want to—couldn't—let go.

The blackness swirled about me. It whispered to keep trying. It nudged me not to quit now. As sure as the owl hooting in the tree goes after its prey—okay scratch that because this was not a predator/prey thing—as sure as the stars twinkled across the heavenly canvas, Michael and I weren't over forever. We couldn't be.

I'd have to earn back his respect, make him care about me. See me in a new light.

Chapter 11

MY ULTIMATE PLAN OF earning back my spot as the twinkle in Michael's eye was harder than I thought it would be, especially when Elena seemed to be judging my every word and move. I longed for the days when Michael sat on the fringes of my circle of friends instead of right in the middle. But no, now I had to watch what I said, smile at the appropriate times, and squeeze in cool *Lord of the Rings* facts whenever possible. Every time Michael nudged me to the side so he could walk with Elena, I was absolutely crushed.

Afternoons didn't help either. I spent time squatting, jumping, leaping, pretending to be a peppy cheerleader. And pretending that the feigned indifference that Jules's friends, especially Ava, showed me didn't affect me.

I caught Jules after practice one day. "Hey, sorry I always gave you a hard time about cheering. It's hard work."

A small half-smile crept onto her face. She released her ponytail so her hair fell in bouncy waves around her. "We know that most don't get it. That's why Ava and I ignore the taunts from girls who are just jealous."

"Why are you even friends with her?"

She blew air out of her mouth at the same time her bag fell off her shoulder. The perfect image of Jules cracked a bit since it was just the two of us. "She's not that bad."

I tapped my foot on the pavement of parking lot. "Yes. She is."

She sighed and threw her stuff in the back seat. Leaning against the car, she said, "You know you're my best friend. But you also know that Ava is too. It's just the way it is. I wish it were different, but you wouldn't want to be friends with her anyway."

"Why are you, if she's such a rotten person?"

"Cassidy." She tried to flash me the message just by saying my name and the cold, hard look that settled on her face.

"I'm serious. What do you see in her?" What I couldn't admit was that over the summer Jules and Ava had drawn even closer. And there was nothing I could do about it.

She grabbed my hand. "Do we have to talk about this?"

"Probably not, but might as well answer."

"Fine. You don't see all the sides to Ava. I know she can be a little mean, but she deals with a lot and has been heavily influenced by her parents just like we have been."

I shrugged. "I guess."

"My turn for a question. Why did you go out for cheering?"

I wanted to stammer out the truth about camp and Zeke, but the words choked in my throat. "Well, you know, it's my senior year and I wanted to round out my experience for college applications." She eyed me with a blank look so I kept rambling. "At camp we learned to see past stereotypes and not to judge, so I thought the best way to understand the life of a cheerleader was to live it."

"Fine. Whatever. You proved a point." Her eyes pierced mine, determination marking her face. "You've probably done that at this point. If you're not enjoying the experience, you can always quit. No one will hold it against you."

I stood in the parking lot long after she'd left, her words stirring thoughts, creating ideas, sparking a plan to solve my problems.

Someone tapped my shoulder. "Hey there."

I whirled around, sucking in a breath, hoping it was Michael. "Oh, hi."

Zeke rubbed his jaw. "How've you been? I mean, outside of our support group."

"Good, I guess." I gripped my backpack.

"You're not even going to ask how my school year is going?" He stuck his hands into his pockets. "Or how I'm managing a new school?"

"Sounds like you're doing fine. Maybe we can talk more later. Okay?" I shuffled away, toward Mom's van. As much as I didn't want to admit it, I missed hanging with him everyday. But if I opened myself up to a conversation right now, I'd end up spilling everything. I was tired, confused, and feeling some major teenage girl angst.

He caught up in a second. "Are you going to homecoming?"

"Yeah, I'll be there." Gosh, I didn't sound very excited. I added some pep to my voice. "I'm a cheerleader."

"Right. I remember." He coughed and covered up what sounded like a laugh.

"What?"

"Oh, nothing." He kicked a stone and sent it flying across the parking lot. "Wanna grab a cup of coffee somewhere?"

This guy was killing me. Everything in me screamed to say yes. Go out. Grab a chance to hang with a friend and forget about life. But what if Elena or someone else saw us together? She'd pick apart my lies in no time. My entire life would unravel. What if in a moment of awkward silence I rambled on about the fact that I hate cheering? Or that my family had no money? I'd lose him as a friend, and I didn't want that.

"How about hot chocolate then? Or just hang at your house?" He persisted.

I stopped and faced him, noticing the way the afternoon shadows hit the scruff on his chin and shadowed his face. I could see why the girls fell for him even though he wasn't your classic good-looker. "I'm sorry. I'm the last person you want to spend time with right now."

I kept walking, giving the clear impression this conversation was done.

He grabbed the end of my coat, teasing, but keeping me from leaving. "Hey, I'll see you next session, okay?"

I tugged my coat out of his grasp. "Definitely."

This time he let me go.

***

ZEKE'S ARRIVAL AT SCHOOL sure made things a pain in the butt for me. So far, he hadn't seen through my half-truths. If he had, he wasn't saying anything. He saw me in my cheerleader outfit on game days. All in all, I was living out a pretty good cover. The most important aspect being that my friends didn't realize Zeke was my summer loverboy.

My mom's van, which somehow I'd miraculously convinced her to let me drive, sputtered to a spot in front of my house. My parents weren't home yet—and Carter was never home after school but often off on one of his many dating conquests.

So why was the front door wide open, drifting back and forth in the breeze?

I stepped out and immediately rubbed my arms from the chill. Leaves skittered across the road, their scraping sound making me jump. I grabbed my key, the sharpest and only weapon I had. On silent feet, I tiptoed up to the door and slowly peeked inside. I shuddered from the creeped-out feeling that fell over me.

Home is a safe place, a shelter, a hideout from the storms of high school and friends and boys and cheerleading. I entered the living room. Everything looked in its place, the plaid couch and matching chair, the antique coffee table, but a feeling hung in the room. It clouded my senses and stirred up fear.

With my pointy key pinched between my fingers and up and ready to strike, I slipped through the downstairs, whipping open closet doors and jumping into the rooms, ready to defend myself. I'd jab the key right into their eye.

After a few moments of deep breathing, I talked myself down from the edge. It was probably one of Carter's groupies, anxious for their turn on the Carter-go-round. They probably found the door unlocked so dug around in his room to steal a copy of his Taylor Swift lyrics or steal a T-shirt or something. That had to be it. Except, Mom was meticulous about keeping the house locked when we weren't home.

I heard a thump upstairs and I found myself fighting off an attack. Breath was scarce and I sucked in air like it was candy. I needed a better weapon than my car keys, so I grabbed a knife from the kitchen, the sharp one that Mom doesn't let me use on anything, not even carrots when I'm chopping them up for dinner.

With a cry, hoping to scare off any intruder, I rushed upstairs like a maniac and ran through the rooms.

They were empty.

My room looked untouched, but when I entered Carter's that was a different story. The whole room was upturned, his clothes spilling out the drawers. I Love You was scrawled across his mirror with red lipstick. Yup this was a result of one of his groupies or a psycho stalker.

This situation was opportunity. I texted Jules instead, begging her to meet with me before school tomorrow morning.

Time to implement my plan.

***

WITH THE BANDAGE ON, I hobbled across the parking lot on crutches my brother used last year. Mom always carries a ton of bandages, and it wasn't too hard to wrap them around my sneaker so it looked like I'd hurt myself.

Jules screeched in next to me and stepped out of her car like she was on a movie set. She leaned against the door with a doubtful expression. Our friendship took a major hit last summer and then again when I invaded her cheerleading territory. But I knew she loved me. She was struggling with guilt. I got it.

"What happened?" she asked.

I rambled on about fighting off an intruder and twisting my ankle when he pushed me down and escaped out the window. She took it all in with understanding nods. Her doubting smile morphed to a sympathetic one that was so genuine I couldn't handle it anymore.

I broke down in the middle of the ridiculous tale. "I'm sorry."

"About what?" She squeezed my hand. "An intruder is scary." She seemed to have forgotten our current tension and that made me melt into a puddle. "I'm sorry things have been so weird between us. Let's hang out this weekend."

"I lied, okay?" I lowered my head, the tears building. "I'm sorry about the whole cheerleading thing and I kinda lied about the intruder. I mean I thought there was one, but it was one of Carter's groupies raiding for paraphernalia." I lifted my head but couldn't get a read on her. "But I never fought him, and...I didn't really twist my ankle."

I thought she'd be furious but instead a smile burst across her face. "Yay! You're back!"

"Huh?"

"My real cousin. The one who tells ridiculous tales because she doesn't know how to get attention or is afraid she's boring and will lose her friends." She smiled. "I missed you. I guess this means you won't be able to cheer?"

My whole life was ripped apart in two sentences. She'd always seen through my stories. Not only that but she saw deeper and understood why. Might as well tell the whole truth. "The hurt ankle is a scheme to capture Michael's attention again...and stop cheering."

She masked her surprise. "I figured it was something like that, but what happened to your dream guy you met at camp?"

I waved her off. "We're going through a cool spell. I think it was the summer heat and bonding of camp that brought us together."

She hugged me. "I'll break the news to the squad that you'll be out for the rest of the season with a bum ankle." Then she whispered, "You might want to switch the bandage to your other foot so you can still drive."

Then she strode into school, confident her cheering life would go back to normal. As she knows, I love sacrificing myself for her but I wanted out of cheering probably more than she wanted me out. The only splits I could handle from now on were ones with bananas.

CHAPTER 12

MICHAEL RAISED AN EYEBROW when he passed me in the hall. "Let me guess, you wrestled an alligator in your backyard."

I sniffed. "For your information..." I was about to mention the intruder and that we wrestled and he pushed me down, narrowly escaping, but the doubt on his face made me realize he wouldn't believe much. "I battled Smaug last night in my backyard. It was epic." I laughed and pointed to my ankle. "I walked away with a sprained ankle. Wish I could say the same thing for the dragon."

He couldn't help but smile at my spot-on sense of humor. "Oh, sorry to hear that." He looked at my bulging book bag and how it swung awkwardly off my arm, and I swear he was just about to ask if he could help. I was so close to getting everything I wanted, because if he asked to help then I could recruit him for the whole day. We could laugh and talk, and I could remind him all the reasons there were to like me, even if I wasn't perfect. This was it. My golden chance shining like a ray of sunshine through a darkened forest. He opened his mouth. "I could—"

Elena flounced between us. "Cassidy! I need your help. I'm about to fail a science test." She sucked in a few shallow breaths, bordering on panic. "My parents will kill me."

"I can help." All his attention went from me to Elena.

Crushed! In a span of five seconds, with one failing science grade, my plan dissolved.

"Oh, could you?" She glanced at my ankle. "Oh, my gosh, you're hurt!"

I waved it off. "Small accident. I'm fine."

"Well, I'd hate to add anything else to your day." She focused on Michael, whose cheeks bloomed. "That would be great if you could help me."

He smiled at me as if that could make up for abandoning me in my moment of need but then he turned and walked away with Elena. As I saw him hang on her every word with rapt attention, I realized what a fatal mistake it had been keeping the never-ending-kind-of-soul-mate-love I had for Michael to myself. Elena never knew his path was not destined to meet with hers, but mine. And it only meant heartbreak for her in the end. Once Michael realized his true love.

Carter bumped into me. "Foiled again, huh?"

I scowled, and it only deepened when Ava appeared at his other side. She barely looked me over, didn't even express sympathy for my hurt ankle or anything. I didn't get a chance to say anything else when she dragged my brother toward her locker.

I hobbled through the halls, thinking my ankle was going to have a miraculous healing in the next couple days...but would be just sore enough that I couldn't finish the cheering season. It's amazing what some ice and a couple days rest can do for a sprained ankle.

At the end of the day, with blisters ripping open on my hands, I slouched in the van, my head on the steering wheel. My life was such a mess.

Someone rapped at the window. I had a terrible feeling I knew who it was. Of course, I hoped it was Michael but I wasn't that stupid—not anymore. I lifted my head to Zeke's smile and his wave. He started in with the hand motions: rubbing his hands together, blowing on them.

I rolled down the window. "You cold or something?"

With a smirk, he said, "That was just to get you to talk to me. Mr. Grabowski sends his regards."

"Oh, was that today?" I usually try to keep up a happy-go-lucky existence, but I had a hard time mustering up even a little bit of cheer.

He cocked his head, his eyes gazing at me with warmth and compassion. "Well, I promised Mr. G. I'd catch up with you, but we can always do this somewhere else. How about over ice cream?"

I hesitated, wondering at the wisdom behind spending time with anyone right now. In my state, I could ramble off anything—probably information I didn't want him to know. I really shouldn't be around anyone right now. But I wasn't going to say no to sugar. "Fine. Get in."

After closing the door and buckling up, he held his hands in front of the heating vent. "Okay, it's cold out too."

"Well, yeah, it's almost winter." My thoughts strayed to winter and all that meant. One, it meant I was part way through my glorious senior year and it wasn't turning out anything like I'd always dreamed. Two, it meant the Christmas dance was fast approaching. Homecoming was just another dance, but at Christmas, the seniors were allowed to take over.

We were silent on the drive over. He tapped his fingers against his knee, and I snuck glances at him. If I only had an ounce of his confidence. Finally, I pulled into *Ye Olde Ice Cream Shoppe* again. A girl with lots of problems to solve can never eat too much ice cream.

I flashed a smile. "How about we share a banana split?" I'd been craving one ever since that morning.

"Sounds good."

Inside, after ordering, we took a seat by the window. I wanted this session to stay away from the topic of me before I could ramble. "I know we're part way through, but tell me how your year is going. Transitioning, okay?"

"It's okay. I'm used to new schools, new faces, new social circles to try and break into."

"Any success?"

He shrugged. "Not really. Not after the initial surge of curiosity."

"Need any tips?"

"Um, sure."

Our number was called. I gestured to my ankle. "Would you?"

"Be right back." He returned minutes later with a grin. "All right. Let's get eating."

It didn't take long and I let him scarf most of it down because it didn't appease my mood like I'd hoped.

"You do know about the Christmas dance, right?" I asked after my last bite of vanilla ice cream, hot fudge and nuts.

"Dance? Like the kind you have to ask a girl to?"

This was serious business. As a newcomer he had to hear it from a girl's point of view. "The Christmas dance is as much of a milestone as senior prom. Way bigger than Homecoming. We've heard about it from upper classmen and older siblings since seventh grade. We waited patiently for our turn to take over the gym and run a dance our way. There's a committee and they can do whatever they want, choose any theme as long as it has some kind of Christmas twist to it."

He nodded solemnly, and I appreciated the lack of mockery. I proceeded to tell him everything a new guy at school needed to know so his date would be happy and fulfilled. "So, if you barely know a girl or if you're not sure how she feels about you, then try to get a group to go together because that eliminates awkward conversation and highly ups your chances of a second date or even a goodnight kiss. Then—"

"I disagree." He took a bite of ice cream then pointed the spoon at me. "I would think that going as a group would decrease the possible romance and thus decrease the chances of a goodnight kiss."

I considered his argument. "I guess that's a risk you'd have to take. If it goes well, you could always get the kiss goodnight on the second date, which is probably for the better, because a kiss on the first date might give the girl the wrong message."

"What if she was expecting the kiss? Then that might give her the message you don't care."

"Ah, yes, but," I scrunched my napkin in my lap, "your text to her the following morning would take care of that. Don't text too early or too late. I'd say right before lunch is good timing."

"Waiting a whole day is best though."

"Fine. Don't take any of my advice and see how well your night goes. I'll be available after when you need counseling. Of course, I might have to charge an—"

"Will you be going?" he asked.

"Going where?"

"The dance?"

I swallowed my nerves. When a guy asks a girl something like that you can't help but wonder his intentions.

"Um," I shrugged, "not sure. Probably." Hopefully, I'd be going with Michael. It was time to make an escape before anymore awkward conversations started. I hopped up again, remembering to favor my left foot. "I need to get home and do more icing."

He held the doors for me and opened the door to my car. Not for the first time, I appreciated that Zeke was my friend.

Once inside, with the engine started, he said, "You can just bring me back to the school."

"Sure."

We didn't talk too much on the way back. I was busy thinking about my next foolproof plan to snag Michael. The chances of attending senior prom with him would go up significantly if I could somehow get him to ask me to the Christmas dance.

CHAPTER 13

FOR MY NEXT ATTEMPT, I got smart.

The whole plan took a couple weeks to devise. With the inept skill that every girl has deep inside, I followed Michael, taking notes on his typical route to and from school. I chose Saturday at nine in the morning, when Michael drove to the library without fail.

Turns out one iced-tea is all it takes. I drank the whole thing first—why waste a good sugar drink? Then smashed it against the side of the road. With precise care, I lay the largest, pointiest shard on the side of the road. It only took ten times for the magical *pop!*

I should've brought hot chocolate and snacks. I should've brought warm clothes—like my snowsuit even though it made me look like a giant puffball. It was only late November, but the air nipped at my face like it was mid-

January and a blizzard was about to hit. Thank God, Michael would drive through in exactly five minutes.

When six minutes came, sweat started leaking from pores I didn't know I had. Maybe I should've swiped his phone to check his calendar. What if he had a dentist appointment? I stood at the side of the road, with the jack pointed under the car. Dad showed me once, walked me through the entire step-by-step process to changing a tire, but that was two years ago. A girl can forget these things.

An old sedan pulled up behind me. I saw the tufts of white hair and wire rimmed glasses and knew my plan was anything but foolproof. The elderly gentleman stepped out of the car. His baggy pants and zip-up jacket looked like he wore them every day. How sweet and so thoughtful to stop and help.

"Need a hand?" he asked, then before I could get in a word edgewise, he rambled on about his granddaughter and how she lives on the other side of the country and how much he misses her.

I coughed, glancing nervously down the road. Michael's blue Civic turned the corner. Full-out panic mode hit hard. I hooked my arm through the old man's and led him back to his car. "Thank you so much for your offer to help but I have a friend on their way. You know, modern-day cell phones and everything."

He twirled the ends of his mustache and didn't look convinced. "It's a little chilly. Maybe I should wait until your friend arrives, just in case."

I held my hand over my eyes and peered down the road. "What about that? I see him now. Thank you so much and say hello to your granddaughter. I'm sure she's absolutely lovely."

With a confused look, the man climbed back in the car. That's when Michael drove right by. My heart splintered to bits just like the broken glass that pierced the tire of my car. Elena sat in the front seat. It had to be her with the flash of blonde hair that zipped by. How did she end up with him? I thought she couldn't stand him. They didn't even notice me on the side of the road.

I turned but the man was in his car, blinker on, and pulling out with a friendly wave.

Totally didn't see that coming.

With all my planning and fretting and extra planning, I didn't make any Plan B or emergency plans in case Michael didn't even look to a girl stranded on the side of the road. Of course, he would've if Elena hadn't been jingling her flashy earrings and smiling her glossed lips at him.

And I thought I'd been so smart when I purposefully left my phone in my locker at school, so I technically wouldn't be lying when Michael questioned why I hadn't called my dad. It was so perfect. And it so perfectly failed.

I slumped down on the edge of the jack and grieved my perfect plan. I pressed my fists into my cheeks causing my eyes to squint and the black-top road in front of me to blur in and out of focus. Colors flashed by every five or ten seconds. It really had been the perfect set up. My dream year and perfect prom experience that used to be so crystal clear faded and grew farther and farther away with every failed attempt to get Michael's attention.

The crunch of glass under someone's foot pulled me from my deep philosophical thoughts of falling in love. The footsteps stopped right next to me, and I peered up into the shining sun that turned the person into a dark shadow.

"Who goes there?" I asked, without much enthusiasm.

"Need some help?" Zeke asked. It had to be him. Fate seemed to want us together or have a good laugh at sticking us together.

"Definitely."

His warm hands closed around mine. Surprise jolted through me, but I didn't pull away. I soaked in the warmth spreading through my hands and reaching the rest of my body, like holding a mug of hot cocoa.

"You're freezing. How long have you been sitting here?"

"Um, not too long." The other fatal flaw was not checking out the weather and picking a warmer day.

"I'll change this for you, but let's get you home first."

I didn't argue. I climbed into his car and rubbed my hands together in front of the heater. The car started with a rumble and he pulled into the increasing traffic.

I gave directions to Jules's house. Might as well live up to the image of being filthy rich he had in his head. After about ten minutes, Jules's house rose before us, the endless windows, levels, and garages. I swallowed my nerves and prayed they were at the country club per their usual Saturday routine.

"Why don't you park here?" I pointed a couple houses down the street. "Dad dislikes cars parked along the road or in the driveway. You know, dirt trailing in on wheels and stuff. He's pretty picky about that stuff."

He pulled over and didn't question the ridiculousness of that concept.

I climbed out. "Well, thanks! See you later!"

He turned off the engine. "Could I use the bathroom?"

"Um, yeah, sure." I walked up the stone walkway with confidence, praying no one was home. I arrived at the front door to find it locked. I jiggled the door knob hoping it would magically open. The humiliation started in my chest and spread outward as I realized I would lose all credibility with Zeke. I let out a sugary giggle. "Oops, it's locked." I spotted Aunt Lulu's prize geranium bushes. "You can always go behind the bushes."

"Seriously?"

I fake-laughed like the best of them. "Course not. Kidding! But stay here. I don't want you to know where the key is and then come back later with your minions and steal our stuff."

He sighed and closed his eyes. I took this glorious opportunity to appreciate his chiseled face, light stubble and pink lips. His black lashes rested on his face. It was too bad Zeke wasn't meant to be my soul mate because he was kinda growing on me.

"Stay here." I sneaked around back and found the spare key hidden in Aunt Lulu's birdhouse.

I opened the backdoor first and peeked inside. The opulence wafted over me, pulling me inside. "Hello?" I held my breath, praying no one would answer.

The echo of greeting bounced back and only silence answered me. I ran around to the front and grabbed Zeke. "Okay, let's go." I rushed him inside and showed him the bathroom.

He stepped out a couple minutes later, but instead of exiting the house, he took his time to study the family pictures on the wall. "Your family really focuses on Jules, huh?"

My confidence withered and I stammered out a lie. "My parents aren't really into photography and we get pictures from them every year for Christmas so they kind of pile up. In fact, that's one reason I'm thinking of taking up photography so there'll be pictures of my family up there. We've just adjusted to it, barely notice the pictures."

"Hmm." He played with his lip ring. "That explains a lot."

"I guess so." As I walked him to the back door, I whirled around before opening it. "Wait. What did you mean by that?"

He made his face a blank sheet, as if hoping I wouldn't figure out the true meaning behind his words. "Nothing much. We can talk about it with Mr. G."

I nudged him toward the back door. "Yeah, right. Well, thanks for the ride home but I'm sure you have lots to do."

"You're welcome. Anytime."

I highly disliked that he hinted my problems stemmed from my parents' obsession with Jules. I was about to launch into a highly developed argument but the front door jiggled. I grabbed his hand. "Let's talk more about this…up in my room. I can get you something to drink for your trouble. Where are my manners?"

I practically dragged him up the backstairs to Jules's room. I always felt like a peon in Jules's house. The luxurious carpet under my feet, the glitter of chandeliers in almost every room, and her room especially. I have one small closet and a dresser. She has a walk-in closet the size of my bedroom.

Voices murmured downstairs. They were back. Excuses ran through my head like mad because it was almost inevitable that they find us. Might as well be proactive. No hiding in the closets with Zeke or stuffing him into the linen closet under threat of death if he talked.

"You know what?" My voice shook slightly. "What was I thinking? The best drinks are downstairs, and my parents don't like me to drink or eat upstairs."

"Then what's the mini fridge for?"

I could've continued in the lame lies but something broke inside me at the ridiculousness of the situation and the whole morning. I mean I was about to explain that we kept the drinks up in our room in fridges but had to drink and eat downstairs. I cracked up, the pressure releasing.

"Are you okay?" Zeke stepped back, his head tilted at the girl completely losing it in front of him.

I calmed down and sucked in some breaths. "I'm sorry." More deep breaths and then I spoke in a calm voice. "I let you think I had a lot of money and that this is my house, but it isn't. It's Jules's. I live in a normal house with parents who make normal incomes. At camp I was just too mad to tell the truth."

He smiled. "That's okay. I kinda figured that out. I was waiting for you because that's what friends do."

"And I'm glad you're my friend." I listened for voices. "Okay, now we have to get out of here." I headed out of the room. At the top of the stairs, I whispered, "Sounds like Aunt Lulu. Just follow my lead."

I calmly walked down the stairs and into the kitchen. "Hi there!" I rushed over and gave Aunt Lulu a giant hug.

"Cassidy. What a surprise, dear. You hardly ever—"

"I know I'm hardly ever here on Saturday mornings, but we needed a change of environment...to study." The blush rose in my face. Aunt Lulu watched us both, her face lighting with understanding.

I opened the fridge and grabbed him a kiwi-lime seltzer water because that's about all Jules drinks and shoved it into Zeke's hand. "Let's head back to my house." I kept talking while leading him to the door. "I never would've understood the effect the Russian revolution had on the country. You're a life saver."

The knob turned under my hand. I whipped the door open.

"Cassidy?" Jules questioned. Ava, Jasper, and Carter flanked her on either side. "Zeke?"

"Um, yeah, I got a flat tire and we were so much closer to your house, so...."

I could feel Aunt Lulu's eyes boring into my back, demanding an explanation for getting my stories wrong. I wish I had the ability to formulate thoughts and judge their effectiveness before I spoke them. That would save me from half the awkward situations I found myself in over the course of my lifetime. "We also had to study Russian economics."

Jules peered past my shoulder and understanding dawned in her eyes. She realized Aunt Lulu was not happy with me. She shouldered past me.

"We're heading to my room. See you later, Cass."

"Sure thing." I tried to telepathically beg her to invite me upstairs but it didn't work any better than it did with Carter. I knew he wouldn't help me. As he walked back, he squeezed my arm sympathetically.

"I'll meet you out at the car," I whispered to Zeke, who got the message and slipped outside.

Then it was just me and Aunt Lulu. Uncle Rudie sensed the coming storm and mumbled about shining up the Porsche. I still didn't turn around, even when she started the foot tapping.

"Cassidy?"

For some reason, my hand was stuck to the doorknob, a mental block or something. I thought about all the different ways this could go from Aunt Lulu pressing charges for breaking and entering so I'd learn my lesson— even though I used the key—to her calling my parents, to who knows what. My whole body sagged as the answer came, silent and deadly, because that's what it would be to me: a slow death by Aunt Lulu. Only one thing would distract her from my lies and my actions.

I bit the inside of my lip hoping to produce a few crocodile tears and rushed over, throwing my arms around her. "Oh, Aunt Lulu." I sobbed into her shoulder with great heaving wailing noises.

Aunt Lulu isn't the most affectionate person, more like a porcupine trying to hug, so she didn't know what to do. "Oh, I've tried so hard and nothing works. I'm sorry I was in your house and with a boy but I didn't know what else to do."

Her hands dug into my arms and she pulled back, watching me with alternate expressions of doubt and doubt.

I poured it on thick, putting on the best puppy-dog look I could muster. "I'm lost, Aunt Lulu. I'm trying so hard to get this guy to like me and there's prom at the end of the year, but it will come so fast. I know it. But everything I do fails."

Technically, everything I'd said up to that point was the truth. I swallowed my pride and threw out the trigger word.

"I need help," I whispered, mustering one more tear to slip down my cheek.

Aunt Lulu's transformation was like watching a cloudy dark day transform into a brilliant sunset with bright pinks, purples, and flaming oranges. She went from a heaving mass of tension and indignation to a shivering mass of compassion.

What had I just done? Carter and Jules must either be shaking their heads or laughing hysterically at me through the ceiling.

With a determined face, set jaw, and eyes of a shark, Aunt Lulu clasped my shoulder. "You stick with me, dear. Aunt Lulu will take care of everything."

Then she embraced me, ready to get to work, thrilled with the chance to transform me. With whatever plan she was concocting, I'd be lucky to have any life at all outside of school and homework before Christmas.

CHAPTER 14

I'D LIKE TO SAY that somehow between November and December and my talks with Aunt Lulu, I'd brainwashed Michael to ask me to the Christmas dance, but alas, no such luck.

Michael was going stag with a group of other kinda cute but geeky guys, who also liked pointy ears and archery. Jules was going with her usual crowd. Carter and Ava and Jasper were included in Jules's little group—don't know how a sweet guy like my brother could put up with Ava for so long unless Jules was right about her and she had some redeeming quality that I had yet to see.

Elena and I decided to go solo together. Two weeks before, we'd walked through the mall, searching the discount racks. Dad had surprisingly given me fifty dollars to find something suitable to wear. Of course, everything I loved was over one hundred.

"What about this?" Elena pulled out a hot pink sleeveless number.

"Um, not quite sure it says Christmas."

She pulled out five more dresses in various rainbow colors, including one tie die with a Christmas tree on the front before she let out an exasperated sigh. "None of these dresses are black, red or green if that's what you're looking for."

I ran my fingers through the spring fling dresses from the previous year. "Then where am I supposed to find one?"

"Gosh, why don't you raid Jules's closet? She probably has dresses with tags on them that she'll never wear, won't miss, and won't even remember she had."

I stammered out a few excuses. The primary one being that I'd never steal from Jules, and I also had a sneaky suspicion that Elena would never keep that secret. But on the inside I was squealing. She was brilliant.

"So who is it you're trying to impress?" she asked.

"No one in particular. Just all the guys who didn't think to ask me. At the dance, they will be regretting that decision."

We finished up shopping rather quickly due to a sudden headache on my part. In other words, I needed time to plan.

It turned out to be easier than I thought. Of course, I blackmailed Carter saying if he didn't help me, I'd video him sleeping in his underwear and post it on the World Wide

Web for every one of his potential girl friends to see, and I'd be sure to pick the most unflattering shot.

Every Sunday afternoon, Jules and her parents go out to this gourmet restaurant where one entrée comes to like fifteen dollars or more, and that doesn't include French fries and a side salad, just this tiny cut of meat. You have to pay extra for anything else.

Carter stood on the lookout behind a geranium bush at the side of the house while I sneaked in and entered Jules's room. Normally, when I'm here, Jules is the star attraction, chatting, laughing and showing me her new clothes from some exotic city. Without her there in the room, the silence fell over me. My heart beat with guilt as I imagined Aunt Lulu's scowl and Jules's look of betrayal.

With a headlamp on—Carter insisted on it—I dug deep into the back recesses of the closet. It was like mining in an old tunnel, hoping for the glint of gold.

My walkie talkie crackled. "All well?"

"There's too many clothes!" I hissed back.

"Whatever. Girls," he muttered.

I fumbled about a bit more then stood back and took in the rainbow of colors. "Genius!" I went right for the black section and found a simple-cut short dress that anyone could've bought anywhere. I could probably find the same dress at Target.

Carter's voice came through with a crackle. "Family is home. I repeat. Family is home!"

I grabbed the dress off the hanger, shoved it in my bag, and slipped out the back door just as Uncle Rudie jiggled his key in the lock.

***

THE DAY BEFORE THE Christmas dance, I stopped in at the guidance office for a session with Mr. Grabowski and Zeke. We suffered through another stale attempt to put us on the right path before we were left alone.

"You know," I said, flopping down in the chair. "I really appreciate our support group, but I'm kinda done with them."

He leaned forward, his face growing serious. "I wanted to give you a chance—"

"I wanted to share a few last tips on the upcoming Christmas dance because guys usually get it all wrong, and there are a few things girls wish they'd get right but everyone's too nervous to just blurt it out, so I'm talking for all girl-kind around the world when I say that—"

"Cassidy..."

I just couldn't answer the question he was about to ask. He probably wanted me to spill my guts about last spring and ask me if I really acted alone, but that was one secret I was carrying to the grave.

"Guys have it so easy. All they have to do is rent a tux that matches the color of their date's dress, but the girls have all the pressure to find a dress that's in style, that flatters her figure, that isn't last year's model, that isn't too expensive, too low-cut, too high-cut, the right color, and most importantly that no one else has the same exact dress. But, of course, you probably—"

"Cassidy!" He broke in, his voice firm and commanding. He smirked in a nice way and shook his head like I'd never learn.

"Sorry," I squeaked. "Just don't buy your date one of those huge, obnoxious wrist corsages where the girl feels like she's wearing a flower bush on her wrist when all she wanted was a single stem rose to put in a vase by her bed."

"Done?"

I sucked in a cleansing breath and blew it right back out. "I think so. Don't ask about last spring, so you can satisfy your curiosity. Because I won't answer."

"Well, then. I guess we're done here." He stood without answering that challenge and held the door. "Don't we have a gym to decorate?"

"Yeah, I guess so. Jules is probably ready to send out the entire football team to find me." His words registered. "We?"

He nodded. "Your cousin is ruthless when it comes down to getting people to do what she wants them to."

Jules had roped me into volunteering for the decoration committee, and Zeke too. In other words, she needed servants to do the grunt work while she sat back and admired her creative ingenuity.

She never liked the non-traditional Christmas dance themes that other seniors had created in the past. She hated the Oldies theme, the Eighties theme, the supernatural theme, the favorite TV show theme—she wanted classic. So she tied it into some artsy idea, sparking enthusiasm until everyone agreed. Really, it was traditional black and white or solid colors with a silver color scheme. I'll be honest. It would be the best Christmas dance I'd been to so far.

Even without a date.

The entire place sparkled with glitter and everything silver and white. Before I left, as I was hanging one of the final strands of icicle lights—though I'd managed to avoid Zeke the entire time—he caught up to me.

He bumped into my stool, making me wobble and almost take a nose dive on the basketball floor. I let out a tiny scream, which earned a prompt scowl from Jules.

Zeke balanced me. "Oops. Sorry about that."

"Right." Before the awkward silence between us could grow, I filled it. "I forgot to ask. Did you take my advice about the Christmas dance like no neon colors and try to go as a group?"

"Some of it, definitely."

"What? Are you going to wear bright pink or something?"

He handed me the next string of lights. "Nah, not sure pink is my color. I was talking about the date area. I didn't ask anyone."

"You've got guts."

He shrugged. "A date will just hold me back. I have no desire to spend all night catering to the whims of some girl."

I tacked up more lights. Wow. He wasn't as shallow as I thought, because that meant he hadn't fallen for Jules or Ava or one of the cheerleaders...unless he was just chicken.

"I probably could've hooked you up with someone from Jules's crowd."

He stepped back. "I would never use you for your social connections, even if I'd wanted to ask one of her little clones." He quickly changed the subject before my surprise could even register.

It feels like anyone who befriends me has ulterior motive. Usually, I just have to wait it out and then the favors start.

"Who are you going with?" he asked casually while handing me more lights.

I flashed what I hoped was a mysterious grin. "You'll just have to wait and see."

He tried to hold it back but let out a snicker. "Going solo too?"

"That's right. I'm a confident teen who doesn't fully rely on a date to complete her night." In other words, Michael had no interest in going with me.

We finished up about thirty minutes later. Jules herded us all out, congratulating us on the best-decorated

Christmas dance in over a decade. I thought about the fact that my plans had failed.

I truly would be alone.

***

THE NIGHT OF THE DANCE, Elena slunk into my room with a doubtful look to hide the surprise. "Nice dress." Even though she'd joked about me raiding Jules's closet, she probably never thought I'd have the guts to do it. She probably hadn't given it another thought. Hence the surprise at my expensive dress.

After trying to mind-control the rising blush, which didn't work, I cracked the window. "Phew. It's hot in here."

Elena rubbed her bare arms. "It's December. It's freezing."

I shut the window. "Shall we get ready?"

Thankfully, Elena never connected her joke with my dress, and we proceeded to do our make-up and take turns doing each other's hair in some kind of twisty up do accentuated by sparkly combs.

Out of the blue, Elena said, "Too bad your hot boyfriend from camp couldn't be your date."

I swallowed and added blush to hide my sudden paling complexion. "I agree. That would absolutely heaven, but you know how it is. Summer romances all come to an end."

"Right." Elena continued to add make-up, letting her doubt and accusation rest between us with just one word. She probably never believed me.

Someday I'd tell her and Jules the truth, just not tonight. I was sure, given my experience at camp, they'd forgive me and understand why I made up the romance out of my anger at Zeke. Though right now, I was having a hard time finding those feelings because Zeke had been nothing but nice since the start of the school year, which was rather odd, considering his strong dislike for me at camp. Maybe it was guilt?

Mom got all gushy and forced us into a zillion different poses for pictures. She rambled on about how later we'd appreciate looking back at the shots. She stood back with the glimmer of tears.

"Mo-om!"

"Right. Sorry." She shook it off.

That's when Carter waltzed down the stairs. I know he's good looking or that's what all the girls tell me, but when he flashed his dreamy smile with his hair slightly more combed than usual, I could see possibly what other girls see.

"Ooh," Elena teased. "Going with Ava?"

"Of course." He leaned in to give Mom a kiss on the cheek. "I'll be back by midnight."

Midnight? He had to be kidding? His charm must work on my parents too, because my curfew was 11pm. "Excuse me?"

Mom gave me the look that brought back the scene from last spring when I was lying to the police and then their talk with me when they sprang the whole Adventure Program thing on me. I didn't question my curfew after that.

As we pulled up to the school along with everyone else, reality hit me that I was wearing a dress I stole from Jules's closet. She'd most likely know this, and I was about to enter into her domain. A wave of nausea overwhelmed me.

"Um, Elena?" She looked back with the school behind her, the outside light making her into a silhouette. "I know we decided not to eat much until after the dance but I need to eat now. I'm going to run through the drive-through for some fried chicken or something."

"Ew." Elena shuddered. "Why would you want to enter the dance all greasy and smelling like fries?"

"No, kidding, right? Maybe I'll just get some mashed potatoes then. I don't want to be partway through the dance, feel light-headed and then pass out just for some guy to think I'm swooning for him. Why don't you go in without me."

It didn't take much convincing for Elena to shrug her shoulders and head toward the school.

"I'll be right back!" I said before the door slammed shut.

I sat in the silence of the car, watching kids of all ages enter the dance. The nervous freshmen were dropped off by their parents. The cocky sophomores swaggered in, thinking more of themselves than they should. The juniors, mature and excited that it was almost their turn to be seniors, strolled in; and then my class. Friends I'd been with since first grade, some I knew, some I never really talked to or tried to get to know. They smiled up at their dates, eyes glittering with excitement. My chest felt hollow like everything that had happened last spring had taken a chunk out of me, having an ever-reaching grasp, affecting tonight too. My throat ached.

Carter arrived with Ava and Jules and her crew right behind. I ran my fingers over my black dress, praying that if she noticed, she'd at least understand my desperate move.

I let my head rest against the steering wheel. After a deep, cleansing breath, I left the warmth of my car and entered the chilly air. When I entered the gym, Ava picked me out and said one thing to me.

"Nice dress." She paused, and I waited for the real reason as to why she'd compliment my dress. I didn't wait long. "Funny, Jules had a dress just like that she'd planned on lending me for tonight. What a coincidence."

I let out a panicked hiccup and then walked away.

CHAPTER 15

THE GYM GLITTERED WITH all the lights and hard work. The romance of it took my breath away. When I saw Michael hovering by Elena, waiting to swoop in and ask her to dance, grief squeezed my heart. Overwhelming sadness fell over me.

While trying not to gaze at Michael and silently hypnotize him to ask me to dance, I stood by the food table manned by parent volunteers and teachers. I watched from the fringes, not quite ready to take that step forward. I chatted with Mr. Troller, my English teacher before it became kinda awkward. Eventually, I just people watched. I felt like a protective bubble encased me, and I could float through without anyone noticing me or wanting them too.

No matter how many times I tried to distract myself, my gaze couldn't leave Michael. Only I could appreciate his attire. The suit coat with patches on the elbow and pleated pants. In true nerd style, he wore the pointy ears as if he was making a statement and no one could force him to change. Another thing I liked about him.

Before parents started talking to me or before I was pegged the complete loser of the dance, I moved among my friends and classmates. When Elena noticed, she pulled me into a circle of friends. I danced, my body moving to the beat of the music. After thirty minutes passed, and Jules didn't shine a big ole spotlight on me and announce me as a thief, I relaxed. I let myself go, and for what seemed like a brief time, reveled in this milestone.

I watched Carter and Ava argue and felt a deep sense of satisfaction. Ava was used to being number one, with boys groveling at her feet. Carter couldn't resist dancing with other girls who batted their eyelashes at him.

That's when Zeke strolled in looking hot in his usual way, something only he could carry off. He stood at the entrance to the gym, peering into the crowds. He craned his neck and took a few steps in, a hopeful look on his face as he searched for someone.

I ducked behind a couple grinding away, my breath stolen. I peeked again at his old school tux with tails, a bow tie and Converse sneakers. He looked way more stylish than the guys wearing a suit coat and tie, probably handpicked by their moms. Very suave and totally hot. It seemed like the more I got to know him, the better looking he became. He waited, bearing up under the scrutiny as if he didn't care if everyone knew he arrived solo.

Maybe he was looking for me.

A bit hopeful, I edged through the crowd, my focus on him, all our time together rushing through my mind, the kind words, the emotion, the caring. I was so close, inches away from approaching him when Ava burst through and sidled up to him. Within seconds they were inseparable and he stopped looking and waiting.

It shouldn't have bothered me because I had rejected his friendship all year even though we'd almost sort of had turned into friends, but watching Ava swing her hips and hold onto him like he was hers dug at me. Or maybe it was the realization that my time, my turn with him had passed, and I had screwed it up out of some sort of stubbornness.

I turned away, contemplating these thoughts, when my phone buzzed in my purse. I stepped into the hall to read what turned into a series of texts.

Leave the dress on the back table of the lab room.

Or I'll tell everyone.

Ava

Goosebumps rose on my flesh. Ava knew to call at exactly the right time, when a slow song came on and when I was vulnerable. Maybe too vulnerable. Even though surrounded by hundreds, I felt alone.

If I left the dress in a classroom, I'd have nothing to wear. Instead of this tiny purse, I should've dragged along my mom's purse, which could fit an extra pair of clothes.

"Want to dance?" a guy from my trig class asked.

"Um, sure." Avoidance works, right?

He placed his sweaty hands on my waist and we swayed back and forth. I tried my best to answer his questions but his Cheetoh breath did nothing for me, and I kept thinking about how to follow the directions and not be arrested for streaking.

After the dance with trig guy, a miracle happened. It's like I was sending off some kind of wave that let all the available guys know I wanted to be detained, that I desperately didn't want to do the task before me.

Finally, I had to say no. After a glance back at Michael dancing with Elena, her blonde hair skimming his cheek, I found the courage to leave because I couldn't handle watching that for the next three minutes. I also noticed that Ava was nowhere to be found.

Normally, Jules would be with me on this. She'd know everything. For some stupid reason I'd felt I couldn't ask her to borrow a dress. I couldn't tell her the truth about Zeke...or maybe I didn't want to? Our relationship seemed normal but somewhere between last summer and Christmas, it had changed. Maybe because I kept waiting for her to tell the truth. Maybe I reminded her of her guilt. Or maybe because I'd stopped confiding in her.

I'd walked the halls of my school every day for years, but with the normal fluorescent light missing and the eerie silence thick in the air, I was spooked. The tiny click clack of my heels echoed and every few seconds I glanced behind me.

With doom weighing on me, I finally reached the science wing. I found the chem lab and slipped inside. The long black tables took on ominous shapes in the dark and everyday objects looked like men with their arms raised, ready to attack me.

Pulse racing, I froze in the quiet blackness, desperate for an answer because I couldn't leave in the dead of winter in nothing but my underwear.

Unless.

I could stand up to her. If not, she would only continue to bug me and have her way with me.

My giving in was only making the problem worse.

My parents and Zeke would be proud. I'd be facing my problems head on and not taking any crap from anyone. What would work best? I could sit on the back table and wait for Ava, but what if a horny couple stumbled in? Or what if she peeked through the window to make sure the dress was there first?

Despite the chill in the room, I slipped out of the dress and into my teacher's white lab coat, which gave me all sorts of heebie geebies. This was the same coat he wore every day and I wasn't sure how often he washed it.

A thump sounded at the door and then it creaked open.

I ducked down, crouched in a ball. Oh my God. Oh my God. Oh my God. Every stupid decision I made ran through my head. I could've begged Elena to come with me. I could've told Carter and dragged him along.

Footsteps sounded across the floor, nearing where I was hidden. I listened and noticed the light tap of shoes.

I popped up. "Hey, there!"

She jumped, but I hadn't been able to make sure it was Ava. A sudden light beamed into my eyes. What if it wasn't Ava? Whoever it was, I wouldn't make it easy for them.

"Just so you know my dad's a cop"—total lie—"and he loves me so if you hurt one hair on my head, he'll hunt you down with my mom's sharpest knives and make you regret ever hurting me."

It was a guy! And he kept moving across the room.

"And the whole football team is on their way down here because I have connections and I told them if I wasn't back in five minutes then to come after—"

"Cassidy?" The guy took the final step toward me, lowering the flashlight. Finally, I could see.

Zeke?

"What are you doing?" His eyes flicked over the lab coat. "And what are you wearing?"

"Oh, nothing. I stained my dress with punch and hoped to find something in here to clean it off with, but then I heard a noise, so I hid." I tried not to groan at the lamest lie I'd ever told.

We stared at each other for a few moments, our faces lit up by his light, like we were telling ghost stories. The dim light touched on the slight down turn of his mouth, the hurt etched on his face.

He masked it quickly and plastered on a smirk. "You know, I have connections. If you really want the thrill of breaking and entering or doing whatever it is you're doing here—all you had to do was ask."

"Thank you for the offer, but, uh, I think I'm okay. I've already dabbled in criminal activities," I shot back. "Anyway, I told you. I—"

"Right. You stained your dress." He sighed. "I saw you leave and wanted to make sure you were okay. But I can see that you're doing just fine on your own so I'll go back to the dance. Sorry to bother you."

His footsteps were fast taps across the tiled floor. With each one I wanted to pull him back into the room and take back everything. I wanted to chase after him and tell him everything, beg him to understand.

Instead I hunkered down in the back of the room, quiet as a lab rat, waiting for Ava to claim the dress.

She never came.

I spent the Christmas dance, which I'd looked forward to since seventh grade, huddled in the back of a classroom, cloaked by darkness and completely alone and feeling like crap. Yes, Mom. Like complete crap.

This whole prank thing had been a game to Ava, and the plan had been to leave me in a dark classroom, missing the dance, while she bopped around with all the guys having the time of her life.

The dance stunk, but the blackest darkness has a way of shining a light into the deepest part of ourselves, burning away all the rubble, and leaving behind the truth.

After two hours I knew I'd been played.

The second half of the year would be different.

CHAPTER 16

UNFORTUNATELY, ON HEARING FROM Jules that I spent most of the Christmas dance in a classroom—not sure how that rumor got spread—Aunt Lulu cracked down on me and got serious.

She turned out to be more of a drill sergeant than I expected. After endless how-to lectures on social etiquette, I was turning into a zombie or some kind of Aunt Lulu drone. I'm sure given any other life, she'd have made the perfect evil dictator who would create miniature clones of herself to do her bidding, every one perfect in a horrifying kind of way.

After every-day-after-school sessions for three weeks, Jules saved me. Aunt Lulu and I sat at their dining room table with straight backs, forks poised, chatting about everything but what really mattered.

Jules appeared at the door. A colorful scarf splashed against the perfect white of her winter coat. She glanced at me in a sad I-miss-you sort of way before forcing a smile. "Mom?"

"Not now, dear." She waved Jules away.

I flashed my cousin what must've been a look of complete desperation. She'd tried on and off with some success to cut our meetings short, but in that moment she must've forgiven me for stealing her dress—if Ava ever bothered to tell her. Or maybe she missed hanging out as much as I did. Recently, the awkward tension had replaced any secret-sharing.

She swept into the room, a summer breeze that carried the scent of hope. "Mom. You're doing such a great job with Cassidy. Our friends are asking why she isn't hanging out with us."

The smile burst across Aunt Lulu's face like she'd just won an Oscar or something. She let out an infectious giggle and clapped. "Really? Don't you dare tease me like this."

Jules nodded emphatically. I nodded too, my head moving up and down like a bobble head doll.

"In fact, Mom, I'm heading out now...."

Jules is so smart in this way. She knew the idea had to be Aunt Lulu's, so she planted the seeds and Aunt Lulu totally got sucked in.

"Well, then Cassidy. Consider your training officially over. Time to practice your new skills in the real world." She ushered me out of my seat, her arm around me as she walked me to the door. "Now if you have any questions or struggles you have me on speed dial. Just duck into the restroom or step outside for a bit of breath air and call me. Though I suspect you'll do fabulous, so we'll stay in touch." She kissed my cheek as Jules dragged me out the door and into my new freedom.

***

JULES AND I CHATTED mindlessly about the latest gossip during the drive to wherever we were going. Basically, we ignored all the important stuff we should be talking about like smoke blasters and boys. I wanted to ask what had changed. Tell her that I wasn't mad at her—okay, maybe a little disgruntled. That I understood a pact was a pact, and could we forget the whole thing ever happened? Minutes later we pulled up in front of this gigantic mansion with a front door complete with a gleaming brass knocker.

Turned out we were at Jasper's house. The brainless, dull, classic good-looking jerky jock. We went down a spiral staircase that led to a fully finished basement complete with cushiony carpet, huge flat-screen television, air hockey table and soda bar.

"You're gaping. Close your mouth." Jules nudged me then burst into the room with her laughter and cheerful presence.

Ava hugged her, squealing, then noticed me. Her eyes narrowed, and I shivered under her icy glare. Ava whispered something to Jules, probably about me, and my cousin must truly be the queen bee, because Ava didn't make one jab at my clothes or lack of style.

She went back to her newest boy toy. Carter and I had talked after the Christmas dance, and he mentioned Ava was kind of a bore and his intention was never to be tied down in a relationship. How ironic that my goal for almost two years had been to have a serious relationship and I completely failed; yet, Carter who wanted nothing more than to be the serial dater and flirt, had found himself in a potential serious relationship.

Then I happened to notice whose ear Ava was nibbling on. I choked on the root beer Jules had stuck in my hand—probably to keep me from saying anything stupid. It was Zeke, in the flesh and blood. He leaned back, laughing, his smile genuine and his whispering and attention on Ava sincere. But what did I care? After being a little stand-offish with this group, I thought maybe he wasn't like Ava. I guess I was wrong.

Someone bumped me. "Hey, there."

It was Jasper. His brown hair was cut clean and neat, almost borderline nerdy but somehow he carried it off. I could practically see my reflection in his teeth; and of course, what girl wouldn't notice the dimples? When I casually took in the rest of his clothes, I noticed that he dressed a bit more geeky than Michael. He had khakis rolled at the bottom with a graphic tee and...wait for it...moccasins. Who wore moccasins?

"Want to see something cool?" He smiled, which lit up his eyes. Most girls would commit their life to him right then and there.

I fought off the blush because I didn't want to appear as one of his groupies who fawn all over him and can barely get out a word in his presence. "Um, I guess?"

Jules laughed. "Oh, please, Cassidy. Don't fall for it! He's just trying to get you to make out with him in the next room."

"What?" I squeaked.

He sent Jules a dirty look. "Don't listen to her. She's just jealous." He seemed to think twice about it. "Would you?"

I choked on my root beer for the second time. "Would I what?" Though I had a feeling I knew what he meant.

He waggled his eyebrows. "Make out." He nudged me and I couldn't help but be drawn to his mouth and wonder. "You and me."

I should've said something cool like *you wish* or *get lost* or *in your dreams* or even *sure, let's go*, but no, that's not what happened.

"Well, I'm not sure about that. A girl can't just go kissing anybody especially when the kissee has a reputation...I mean not that you have one, but sometimes I hear stuff, and I mean really reputations are probably complete lies and mean absolutely nothing when in fact you're probably a great guy and wouldn't hurt a flea." I took a deep breath but couldn't stop as he raised an eyebrow with the start of a grin creeping onto his face. This just made me talk faster. "Plus, there's all the girls at school who are waiting for you to ask them out, and I don't want to be known as a heart breaker though who knows? That might be better than my current reputation, and I've learned more than anybody that rumors can be brutal and start from a place of envy..."

Honestly? I ran out of breath. At this point I prayed, desperately, begging God to complete a miracle and open the floor to swallow me, because I was pretty sure I could never show my face in school again. I peered through my lashes, expecting everyone in the room to be listening and staring at me, but they weren't. In fact, they acted like they hadn't heard a word.

His grin turned into a full-out smile. "I'm not sure which one of us has the worst reputation."

I snorted. "Obviously..." I was going to say that he definitely had the worst reputation. Then I thought about the whispers and rumors about proms and rides in cop cars.

"What were you about to say?" he asked, his voice serious even though I couldn't miss the gleam in his eye.

"Obviously, I have the worst reputation."

He laughed, loud and long, and that's what drew everyone's attention to me. Ava still looked suspicious, like I must have bribed someone like Jasper to have him laugh at anything I said. Jules smiled and winked. Zeke completely ignored me, but seemed bothered as he asked Ava to play some car racing game on the video game system.

Jasper leaned into me. "I kinda like you."

I smiled shyly. I'll admit it. I'd have to be an unfeeling zombie to not have a major case of the flutters when the hottest, most popular guy in school said he liked me. Even if it was only kinda.

"How about we go outside and give them something to talk about?" He nodded toward the door that led to an outside patio. "We can kiss if you want, or we can just let them think we are. It could improve your reputation. I promise I'll keep you warm."

I was going to say no maybe some other time, except Elena flounced into the room with Michael trailing behind her. She caught one look at me and seemed surprised, like how did I end up here before her? Michael took note of me too, especially since Jasper was still whispering in my ear. A deliciously warm feeling accompanied his words, and I felt like I was floating.

What if Michael was jealous? What if I had been going about this all wrong? I glanced at Jasper sideways. He grinned, offering me the chance I was looking for.

"Why not?" I asked.

He hooked his arm through mine and led me from the room amidst the cat calls. Jules's voice rose above the rest. "You hurt her and I'll rip your balls off, Jasper!"

"Yikes. I'd better behave." He grabbed my hand and led me to the swinging bench seat.

"It's freezing out here." I rubbed my arms and jumped up and down.

"That's the point." He pulled me into his lap and wrapped his arms around me, his chest pressed against my back. The guy was like a wood stove.

"Man, you're hot," I said, my breath forming small clouds, then immediately wanted to bite back the words. "I mean, you know what I mean." I stopped before I could start rambling again.

"No, I don't. Why don't you explain?" He ran his fingers through my hair with gentle touches.

"I mean your body is so hot, wait, I mean you produce a lot of warmth."

But he laughed, and didn't hear the second part of my sentence. When he stopped, I repeated myself.

"I got it. No need to cover."

I gave up. With his lips so close to mine, I was tempted. This was the situation where if Michael truly loved me or even liked me a little, he'd burst through the door and come up with some excuse why we had to leave. Then he'd stride over and pull me from Jasper's lap and whisk me away. But there must be rules to making a guy jealous, especially when it comes to kissing.

What if Michael came out and caught us kissing? He could totally lose faith in me, think I'm a slut and never talk to me again. Or if we were just about to kiss, he could feel like the rescuer, saving me from myself, before I kissed the wrong guy. But a girl can't stay in the position of the almost-kiss without being a tease and losing the potential to make her guy jealous in the future. These difficult choices were running through my head, when Jasper brushed his lips against the corner of my mouth. It would've been so easy. I could tell Jasper would be a good kisser.

Then the door opened and I sucked in a breath, shocked that my fantasy was about to come true. Maybe I'd misread Michael? Maybe he was using Elena to make me jealous?

Zeke walked through the door, his eyes zeroing in on me right away.

CHAPTER 17

HE RUSHED THROUGH THE door with Ava hot on his heels. She tagged along with more than a scowl on her face. Not many guys have the guts to leave her when she's weaving her love spell over them.

That's something that completely baffles me when it comes to girls like Ava. They're drop dead gorgeous, built in all the right ways with the shimmery golden hair and lots of money to go along with it. They swing from the top of the social totem pole and have gotten so used to it that it turns them into a snob, even if to start with they were nice girls— like me, of course.

So why would Ava rush after Zeke when it just made her look weak, pathetic and needy? I had no clue. Maybe someday I'd figure that out along with everything else like world peace and poverty and how to make cafeteria food edible.

Zeke stood across the deck, his stance like a warrior, fire in his eyes.

Jasper whispered, "I think your boyfriend's mad."

"He's not my boyfriend," I whispered back.

"Could've fooled me."

Ava continued to babble on excessively about how freezing it was and if she stayed out too much longer than the gel in her hair would freeze and she'd look like an icicle. Zeke completely ignored her, much to my growing pleasure, as he moved forward again, his legs swallowing up the distance between us. When he stopped, he seemed to muster any control he had. He breathed deep, rolled his shoulders, and cracked his neck.

Then with a tight smile, he said, "Wanna get out of here?"

I didn't like the little-girl feeling I had right then, and Michael hadn't even started inching away from Elena and toward the deck. "Well, I'm not too sure about that. I just got here..." I took another peek. Still no movement from Michael. "What's so important?"

"I'd rather not say aloud, but we have stuff to talk about."

Here's the problem with going to that kind of camp where you meet a boy your age: He feels like he knows everything about you, and then he starts attending your high school.

"We could stop for ice cream too." He said it like he was holding a brand new shade of lipstick in front of Ava.

In that moment it was like time froze. Michael flirted with Elena on the other side of the sliding glass door. Ava stared intensely at the back of Zeke as if to will him to look at her. Jasper's lips were inches from mine, teasing, waiting for what he always gets. Zeke had his eyes on me, waiting for an answer.

For the first time in my life, I was the power player. I had the option to make a short-term sacrifice to reach my long-term goals. I mean someone like Jasper wouldn't be interested in someone like me for very long. I was just a new challenge, a fresh breeze that happened to blow in his direction and capture his interest for a few minutes.

But what if I blew him off? What if I used Zeke to get my revenge on Ava and make Jasper jealous, so he'd pursue me and then in turn make Michael jealous? Of course, it could be social suicide, too, but...

"Know what? I think I'll take you up on that." I plastered on a smile and leaped from Jasper's lap, leaving his puckered lips in the cold. I hooked my arm through Zeke's, and we whisked back through Jasper's basement.

"Sorry, Jules. Sorry everyone." They all looked up. "We're heading out."

Jules narrowed her eyes but smiled approvingly when she saw I was with Zeke. Suddenly leaving with the popular new guy made my actions more acceptable. Michael gave a cursory glance, but then went back to his awkward flirting with Elena.

Poor guy. He still didn't realize he was with the wrong girl.

We were at the door when Jules said, "Oh, by the way, Cassidy, you'll have to join prom committee!"

"Sure thing!" Then Zeke and I left.

Prom? I fought a wave of brief discouragement because I didn't see how—through all these smoke and mirrors and games, I'd ever end up with my dream date at prom.

***

"SERIOUSLY?" I WANTED TO add more than that but I couldn't say everything coursing through my mind at that moment. Not if I wanted to use Zeke to make Jasper jealous to make Michael jealous so I could have my dream prom date.

Zeke had pulled into a roller skating rink. "What?"

I pointed to the Fun Times Rink sign. "This is what you dragged me away for?"

"Definitely. You never want to appear desperate with that group, and by staying just long enough to be grateful, but not so long that you annoy them, you're doing good."

I still doubted. "Fine, whatever." Too bad Jasper wouldn't be around to see us. Maybe it was better that I'd left him wondering.

Let's just say that roller skates and I were not meant to be best friends. I wobbled precariously around the rink and fell on my butt at least once a minute. It didn't help that all these cocky little kids were zooming past me like this was the freeway and I was some kind of grandma driving her old Chevy. After my tenth time falling and after the fact that my butt was done kissing the floor, I skated off and fell into a seat with a sigh of relief. I wasn't sure how long I sat, dazing off and oblivious to the party horns, music and cake.

At some point, Zeke plopped down next to me. I expected him to say anything except what he did.

"I wasn't exactly Mr. Nice Guy at the Christmas dance. Maybe it's time we call a truce."

A truce? That meant friendship and texting and telling the whole truth about last spring because that's what friends do.

The last thing I wanted to do was hurt his feelings, but if we became true friends then I'd feel bad about the half-truths and eventually break down and spill the truth about last spring...and I couldn't go there. "I'm sure we could be the best of friends, but you saw Ava back at Jasper's. Ava is my cousin's best friend. If I all of a sudden become best buds with you when she's going after you?" I drew my finger across my neck. "Social suicide." Disappointment flickered on his face. "Not that I care about what Ava thinks, but I do care about my cousin."

Just like that all my plans to use Zeke to make Jasper jealous to make Michael jealous fell apart, but I was right. If I crossed Ava, what would she do to me? I'd have to leave Zeke out of the equation and just use Jasper in my nefarious plans.

He laughed. "I never suggested we should get married. We can be friends without flirting and hanging all over each other all the time, right?"

"Right." I fiddled with the laces on my skates. Something scared me about being real honest-to-goodness friends with Zeke. I didn't even know what.

"Then it's settled. We're friends. And friends don't let friends give up."

"Huh?"

He grinned and his eyes lit up in a way that would make most girls swoon or at least want to be his friend. I needed more smiles like that in my life.

He grabbed my hand. "Let's go. One time around."

"Oh, no way." I yanked my hand back and gripped onto the chair. "Forget it. My butt's on strike."

He laughed and after prying my fingers off, pulled me to my feet. "Let's go."

On the floor, he skated backwards and held my hands. He swayed back and forth. "Just one foot and then the next. Glide forward."

I wobbled and let out a little squeak—okay more like a loud squeal. He steadied me. "Don't look at the floor." He lifted my chin. "Look at me."

For the next few minutes I gazed into his lovely greenish-brown eyes that were focused on me. He asked me questions. How'd I do on the science test? Do I like bunny rabbits? What's my favorite color? Where was I applying to college? Had I made a snowman yet this year?

When he ran out of questions, a comfortable silence fell between us. I became aware of things like the sound of our breathing and the smell of his laundry detergent and how nice his touch felt. My insides did this twisty little dance.

"We've been around at least ten times. I've done more than a sufficient job at not giving up so you've done your friendship act for the day."

He led me over to the benches. We switched over to sneakers and bought French fries before heading out. The conversation was easy and I thought just maybe this whole friendship thing could work.

I had him drop me off at home. He pulled into my driveway but kept his hands on the steering wheel. "I had fun. Thanks."

"I did too," I said softly. "Thanks."

He flashed a smile then held up his fist. "Here's to friends."

"Right, friends." Then I fist bumped him as the official start of our friendship.

I opened the door, shivering at the brisk winter wind. I watched his taillights turn the corner and sighed. All my plans have incredible potential and are brilliant in and of themselves, but sometimes I have no control over outside elements.

Like other boys.

CHAPTER 18

THE SECOND PROM COMMITTEE meeting, I purposely arrived early so I could snag a seat close to the door. That was key. I wore my favorite skinny jeans, wondering how many times I could wear them before others started to notice.

A variety of kids shuffled into the room. I could tell by their faces why they were there. The kids with a sullen look, their eyes blank and staring, had parents who had highly suggested they join any and every committee to add to their college applications. They sat like robots, ready to receive their assignment or just sit through Jules's speeches and show up to decorate the night before.

Some girls came in like they just walked out of a salon, their hair extra curly or fluffy and lipstick expertly applied. Those girls wanted something. Either an in with the popular crowd, or they were trying to catch the eye of a boy. I guess, technically I was in this category except I did *not* fluff my hair.

Then there were the people who actually cared, like Jules and Ava and some of their other friends. Of course, the boys in their group showed up under threat of death.

Jules showed up with bright eyes, an enthusiastic smile and stacks of clipboards, sign-ups, and handouts. At the first meeting, we'd filled out a survey that would help her figure out our best skill set. Today, we'd find out who we would work with and on what.

Jules rang a tiny bell to get everyone's attention. She stood tall and proud, smoothing the ends of her scarf. "This is going to be the best prom this school has ever seen. And thanks to all of you, we're going to make this happen. In ten years, teachers will still be talking about this prom." She squealed and clapped her hands. "And you're going to be a part of this."

Oh, yay. That's what I thought, but I had to admit a tiny part of me was excited. Jules has that effect on people.

Still, while she yammered on about the different categories and subheadings and sub-subheadings of what needed to be done, I studied Jasper, wondering if he'd be willing to make some sort of deal. Even when he wasn't smiling, the faint indentations of his dimples could be seen. He wore the moccasins with rolled up khakis again, and I swear, some day, I'd ask him how he got away with this fashion faux-pas. Then there were his lips, soft, pink, and slightly parted like he wanted girls to notice how kissable they were. Well, it worked.

Someone kicked my chair. I glanced back at Zeke, who studied me, his lips slightly curled, but I couldn't tell if they were curled in an almost smile or a smirk, like he knew I'd been checking out Jasper.

"What?" I mouthed.

He shrugged as if to say nothing and then pointed back to Jules like we should be paying attention.

Jules kept talking and talking and talking. I didn't realize there were so many complicated aspects to prom. I mean, it was a dance, not a scientific experiment for the Nobel Prize. I was excited and looked forward to prom just like any other girl but lately I'd been having doubts and realized that along with prom came a whole lot of other issues, like dates and dresses. If I'd learned anything from the Christmas dance, it was that not everything goes our way or ends in a fairytale happily-ever-after way. I raised my hand.

Jules jabbered on until finally, she paused, then said, "Cassidy?"

"Why does this all have to be so complicated? It's about a guy and a girl and a dance. This isn't some fairy tale."

Silence fell over the room. A minute went by while Jules tapped her finger against her chin, obviously deep in thought. The whispers started and chairs shifted.

Zeke whispered, "You've done it now."

I even got a glance from Jasper. Was that a gleam of respect in his eyes for me? I decided to act on that. "I just think sometimes simple is best like when writing a paper for English. When we add too many details or adjectives it muddies what we're trying to say and our grade goes down, but if—"

Jules finally moved and clapped her hands. I stopped talking, fearing the worst.

"You. Are. Brilliant!" Except on the word brilliant she couldn't stifle the tiny scream of excitement and it sounded more like brill-eeeeh! "That is the best idea ever!"

Ava whispered in her ear, and Jules spun, whispering back with many animated hand motions and facial expressions. A smile spread across Ava's face, and I wondered what I'd said right.

With a huge smile, Jules faced the prom committee. "We were going to take all next week to brainstorm themes for this year's prom, but we don't have to. All thanks to Cassidy."

You could've heard my heart punching against my ribcage. No one understood, including me.

"A guy and a girl. A fairytale prom. Simple." She punched the air. "That's it! A fairytale theme, complete with a castle, a bridge, a moat and, of course, princes and princesses at the ball!" She started going off on rabbit trails and ways to incorporate this theme into the rest of the year.

"And Cassidy, you're heading up the decoration sub-committee. Choose someone to help, and let me know if you need more."

Perfect. After the meeting was over, I'd get Jasper to help, hinting that I could use his big muscles. He could never resist the chance to flex in front of other people, even if it was just himself.

But then Zeke spoke behind me. "I'll help her."

"Thanks, Zeke. That would be perfect." Jules smiled warmly at us. "It shouldn't take up too much of your time, and a lot of it can be through email or texting."

I tried not to scowl. It was like everyone knew about my secret plan to use Jasper to make Michael jealous and had decided to go out of their way to squash my efforts. I had a deal to make with Jasper, the offer of a mutual partnership where we could both help each other out. Strictly a business relationship.

When the meeting ended, I decided to follow Jasper out to the parking lot and share my proposal with him there, but then Jules asked to chat with me and Zeke. Turned out she wanted to be kept up to date on our plans so she could approve.

Every time I tried to talk to Jasper the next few days, it was like he had hired a flock of girls to be his body guards, because I could never break through to say hello or wave.

Finally, I got desperate.

Friday morning, I planned my outfit down to the tiniest details, like the short skirt and dangly earrings. Later that day, I skipped World Studies, and slipped into the boys' bathroom in the math wing. It wasn't hard to figure out Jasper's schedule. His entourage had it memorized. All I had to do was walk behind them in the hall a few times before one of them let slip something about what class he had next.

In the bathroom, I waited in a stall, just in case some other boys walked in, which they did. I sat up on the toilet with my feet up against my chest so the guys wouldn't see my girl shoes. A couple of them tried to open the door. I held my breath and waited for them to leave. Finally, I heard the gentle swish of moccasins on the tiled floor. I freshened my lip gloss and walked out of the stall before I caught Jasper in an awkward position.

He was surprised for about three seconds, then took it in stride. "Hey, there, Cassidy. What's up?" Like girls approached him in the bathroom all the time. Who knows? Maybe they did.

I jumped up on the windowsill, tugged on my skirt, and crossed my legs. Gosh, how do girls manage wearing short skirts all the time?

He leaned against the wall, one leg crossed in front of the other, his hands in his pockets like he was posing for a magazine shoot. How did he do it? Something about his confidence unnerved me and I forgot my practiced speech. I should've brought note cards.

"You're cute when you're nervous." He tilted his head, his smile seductive.

"I'm not nervous just, um, well, anyway, how's senior English?"

The door partially opened. Jasper called, "Occupied!" The door shut. Geez. Talk about power. "What do you mean?"

Clearly, he hadn't expected me to talk about schoolwork. "Well, I happened to notice that you struggle a bit in that class and I thought we could help each other out."

A full-blown smile spread across his face that said he loved my idea. "What're you thinking?" He closed the gap between us, and I suddenly found it hard to breathe. He rested his hands on either side of me and brought his face right in front of mine. "What do you want from me?"

Gosh, did girls approach him in the bathroom all the time? I thought he'd be outraged or offended, but I didn't expect this. "I've had my eye on a certain guy and even though I've tried other methods of getting him to notice, they've all failed, so I thought maybe..."

"You're even cuter when you ramble."

I sucked in a breath. "Really?"

He nodded. "Yeah."

"Wow. No one's ever told me that," I whispered. Then I noticed the tiny almost invisible freckle right above his lip.

"It's about time someone did." He peered into my eyes like they were a deep pool and he was testing the waters. "Let me guess. You need my help in making the guy jealous."

"Uh-huh."

His breath mingled with mine as he whispered his next words. "And you'll write my papers for a date once a week."

"Uh, huh."

He brushed his lips against my cheek. "I'm all yours, Cassidy."

"Uh, huh."

Then his lips were on my ear, and I felt this floaty feeling overtake me like my fairy godmother had put me in a bubble. He whispered. "Get ready to have a lot of fun."

Then he was gone.

"Uh-huh."

Chapter 19

I SAT WITH ZEKE on one of our support group meetings. We didn't meet as frequently anymore, and as much as I wanted them to end, it was a great excuse to spend time with him.

"Cassidy?" he snapped.

"Um, what?"

"What do you think about that?"

"Well, considering, I mean, um, yeah, it's a great idea." The words all came out in a rush, and I ducked my head so he wouldn't see the obvious blush. I had no clue what he'd said. My first date with Jasper was that night!

He laughed, then leaned forward. "Can I ask you a question?"

"I might not answer."

"If you don't like attention then why did you bring all that stuff to the Program?" His laughter had faded, and the look in his eyes was so intense and caring, nothing like most people's when they ask me questions about stupid stuff I do. Mostly, people are just curious or nosy or want fresh gossip.

"I was desperate and hoped that I'd get kicked out."

He smiled slightly, revealing his crooked teeth that were growing on me. "Why would they kick someone out for breaking the rules when it was a program for teens who break rules?"

"I sometimes do stuff before thinking. It's not about trying be a rule breaker or rebellious or get the attention of my parents or make some big statement."

"Then what is it about?"

I opened my mouth to answer then caught myself— thank God! "I see what you're doing. Nice one, counselor." I waggled my finger. "Shame on you, taking advantage and trying to get me to reveal my deepest secrets."

He shrugged. "Isn't that why we're here?"

"No! We're here to please my parents and the school and everyone else who thinks I have behavioral issues, so they'll let me graduate. When really I'm like any other teen. I just get caught."

He nodded. "Fair enough. You might want to think—
"

The door opened and Jules popped her head in. "Do you guys have a minute?"

"Sure," Zeke said dryly, "It's not like we were talking about anything important."

"Oh, good." She dragged an armchair over and joined our cozy group, which I found oddly appropriate since technically she should be the one sitting in this room with me. "Have you guys been brainstorming decoration ideas at all? I've barely had a minute to catch up with you."

Zeke winked at me. "Cassidy said something about dressing up on Valentine's Day."

"I did?"

Jules giggled but then her eyes widened and excitement spilled out like she was an alien with an internal lighting system. It practically shone off her face. "Zeke! You're a genius."

"Yeah, I don't think so!" I snorted.

"Calm down, Cassidy. It could be a disaster with the wrong costumes, but...what if you two dressed as a medieval knight and princess on Valentine's Day and delivered the carnations?" Her excitement bubbled over and—I'll admit—was contagious. "This would be the perfect segue into our prom theme!" She clapped, did her little squeal thing, told us she'd be in touch and was gone, leaving behind the faint trace of her fancy perfume.

Zeke broke the silence as the shock of what Jules wanted us to do sank in. "Is she always such a whirlwind?"

I nodded. "Yeah. She gets it from her mom." I swallowed, trying to coat my throat, which had gone dry at the prospect of dressing like a medieval princess for a day. "Valentine's Day is next week, isn't it?"

***

WHEN I GOT HOME, I put to the back of my mind what I had to do next week, because I had a date to get ready for. Jasper was picking me up at six.

Honestly, if I'd thought this through, I would've realized the greatest flaw about this plan. Me on a date with Jasper. The king of the crowd. The guy everyone wants. What if I said the wrong thing or heaven forbid starting rambling on and on about my life and totally bored him to the point where he couldn't take even one more date with me? Because that *could* happen.

Desperate times called for desperate measures. I knocked on Carter's door.

He opened the door a crack and one eye peered out. "What do you need?"

"Well, you see, I have a date tonight, and I could use a guy's opinion."

"Wear clothes, maybe some lipstick, look like yourself and try not to talk too much." Then he shut the door.

"It's with Jasper."

Carter flung open the door and yanked me inside. "How did you get a date with him?" As he spoke, his thumbs flew across the keyboard of his phone, texting. He finished and threw it on his bed.

I glanced at the mound of duct tape on his bed. "I know all that stuff has to do with a girl, but it's looking kind of suspicious."

He shrugged, but he couldn't hide the gleam of excitement in his eyes. "You'll find out when everyone else does. Nothing illegal. Don't worry."

I flopped on his bed. "I don't know what to wear."

"Don't worry. I took care of it." He pulled me off his bed and pushed me toward the door.

"Wait! What do you—" Then I was in the hallway and my phone was ringing.

It was Jules. She squealed that I had a date with Jasper and ordered me to my closet. I described my clothes and she said no to everything until my entire closet was on the floor.

"There's nothing left."

"Hang tight. I'll be right over."

Forty-five minutes later, Jules had me ready for my date. Again, we'd spent the whole time focusing on everything but what really counted. I missed talking to my cousin.

I looked in the mirror, not sure what to think, but I didn't want to disappoint her. She'd brought over a bunch of clothes and she'd settled on a shirt with so many ruffles I looked like Big Bird, with black skinnies and what looked like pirate boots. She put on my make-up, mascara, lipstick and everything. Then with a kiss and whisper of "Go, go get 'em" she whisked out the door.

I sat in my room, keeping an eye on the street, watching for his headlights. I couldn't bear to look in the mirror at the mini-Jules she'd turned me into. Maybe I could find something in my closet...I heard a car outside. Too late. It would take me at least half an hour.

I trudged toward the top of the stairs. Carter opened the door to his bedroom and whistled in approval.

"Thanks." I hesitated. "It's not too much?"

"Nope. You'll have the guys drooling."

Great. Not sure I wanted that much attention. Jasper had arrived and Dad was chatting with him. Everything else was forgotten.

"You'd better go," Carter said.

After taking a deep breath, I launched myself down the stairs, gushing, out of breath, already babbling like some kind of wish fountain. I stepped in between Dad and Jasper. "Dad this is Jasper. Jasper this is Dad. Okay, we gotta go."

"Whoa! Wait a second, young lady." Dad put a halt to my hasty exit. "I just want the chance to meet your date. After all, I don't get this opportunity very often."

Great Dad. Way to embarrass me. But it turned out I didn't need help in that department because when they shook hands, I cringed. Jasper's expression had crinkled into confusion. He'd looked at me like he expected someone different.

This was all a big terrible mistake.

At the last minute, I rushed into the bathroom. Without thinking through anything, just desperate, I grabbed

Mom's sewing scissors jammed in a kit in the linen closet and was about to slice off some ruffles when I remembered it wasn't my shirt. What was I thinking?

I gripped the sides of the sink and took in several deep cleansing breaths, which did absolutely nothing for the rising level of panic. The answer came. I'd just hide my shirt. Simple. I sidestepped out of the bathroom to the closet where I grabbed the largest coat, which happened to be Mom's, and slipped it on, covering the shirt.

Dad gave me a curious look, but I slipped my hand into Jasper's and sighed in relief as we stepped outside and the darkness of night hid me like a shroud.

Miracles happen. I didn't talk for the first three minutes of our car ride. We zoomed through the streets of our town in a car that felt like a spaceship.

Jasper turned off the radio. "So who's this guy you like and what do you want me to do other than make him madly jealous when my hands are all over you at the party tonight."

"It's Michael Greenwood. And whoa. I don't think so. This isn't some free grabfest." I flashed him my don't-mess-with-me look, which I didn't even know I had. "You might get away with that with other girls but not with this one."

He smiled, his cocky grin that he usually wore at school. "Seriously, I'm just telling it the way it is. Nothing makes a guy more jealous than seeing a girl he can't have."

"Well, I don't think that will work with me. Instead, I want to walk in with you so everyone can see we're together. Then, later, casually like it was a complete accident, bump into him and share good stuff about me that would make him jealous."

"Like what?"

"Well, anything would work whether it's the truth or not, because right now I couldn't look any worse in his eyes than I do right now."

Jasper whistled. "No problem." He saluted. "I'm yours for the night."

At the party, he walked inside with his arm around my shoulder and within three steps of entering the house, he had his lips on mine. He whispered, "That's just the start."

He let go of me to bump fists with his friends. To me it felt like the blaring music and the chatter stopped, and a wave of whispers started. My temperature skyrocketed especially in my mom's coat. She has okay style. It was more that it was meant for zero degrees and I was inside a stuffy house packed with people.

He mentioned something about grabbing us a drink and then he left me stranded. I drifted through the crowds, apologizing when I bumped someone's arm and their drink spilled, but the coat added an extra three inches I wasn't used to.

But if I took it off, I'd be the Ruffle Queen.

I caught glimpses of Jules and Ava dancing and laughing, making the whole party scene look so easy, so natural. Carter winked and hid a smile, his arm draped over his latest date. I began to wonder if this night would completely fail, because I hadn't seen Michael or Elena yet.

I moved into the hallway to escape the crowd and ran into Michael. I turned, heat flooding my body. This was a big mistake. Making a guy jealous was one thing, but letting him see you as Big Bird was completely different.

"Cassidy?" he asked.

"Um, yeah?" I zipped the coat down a tiny bit to let in a cool draft. My frills-for-days shirt was sticking to my back, and I desperately needed to take this behemoth coat off.

"What are you doing here?"

I flipped around. "What's that supposed to mean? I'm just as surprised to see you here."

Michael's eyes widened as he took me in. "I mean, I don't usually see you at this scene."

I leaned against the wall and twirled my finger around a lock of hair, trying to copy a typical Jules move. "Maybe you've just missed me."

The bathroom door opened and Elena sashayed out. Michael immediately dropped out of our flirty conversation. "Hi, Elena."

She smiled, her whole face lighting up like she truly was glad to see him. "Oh, hi, Michael. Nice party, huh?"

Michael's head bobbed up and down. "Definitely."

"Oh hi, Cass." She pulled me down the hall and whispered, "Can you believe it? I never thought we'd be friends, but he's kinda cool." She tapped her chin. "I guess, in part, it's thanks to you."

"Huh?" There was no way I pushed the two of them together. Even if it was just a friendship.

"I think it all started when you hurt your ankle and Michael helped me pass my science test." She smiled. "It started slow but soon after Christmas just took off." She leaned forward and whisper-giggled. "I even like his pointy ears."

She turned back to Michael. "Wanna get a drink?"

"Sure!"

Together, fast friends, they left the hall and re-entered the party. I slipped into the bathroom, trying to control the rising panic attack and then happened to glance at the mirror.

I almost dropped dread. My hair was curling and frizzing in spots. My face was the color of over-ripe tomatoes and my eyes were glassed-over. I slipped the coat off and opened the bathroom window. The cold breeze wafted in with the smell of snow and I breathed a sigh for the first time the whole night. The sweat dried and I tried to forget about Michael and Elena and my aching heart.

My eyes fluttered shut as I leaned on the windowsill, dreaming about a perfect world where my soul mate wasn't falling for one of my friends.

Not sure how long I sat there when voices drifted my way, catapulting me from my fantasy. My heart leapt into my throat because it was Jasper and Michael. Maybe the poofy coat thing was a blessing after all. Lucky for me, they were talking outside on the deck, right next to the window, and I had a front row seat.

"Yeah, man, she's the most interesting girl I've met in a while," Jasper said.

"Really?"

I frowned because Michael didn't sound convinced. I hoped Jasper had more ammunition than that or he was the worst liar ever. No wonder he was an awful writer. No creativity.

"Gosh, yeah. We have the best conversations about football..."

I kept myself from groaning. It felt like someone punched me in the gut. What if this whole plan backfired? Clearly, I needed to give Jasper a teleprompter. I kicked myself for not telling him about Michael's interests or at least giving him some ideas. I'd just told him to lie.

Michael interrupted him. "I'm going to get back to the party."

"But wait, have I told you how good she is? You know..."

Right there I died on the spot. I didn't need to imagine what gestures went with those words.

"Cassidy isn't like that. She might be a little eccentric but she's not like *that*," Michael stated.

My spirits soared. Michael stuck up for me! He'd defended my honor!

Just to prove himself, just to follow my directions, just to get that A on a paper, Jasper went into detail about how good I was—in the kissing department, of course.

Any thrill at Michael defending me faded, and I slid down the wall until I was sitting in a miserable heap of humiliation. So much for this night. I'd had enough.

I marched back into the party before Jasper or Michael could come back inside, not caring that I still looked like a tomato, not caring about my shirt. I grabbed Elena and pulled her to the side.

"Will you tell Jasper I had to go?"

Elena studied me. "Are you okay?"

I blinked back the tears building fast and furious. "I'm fine. Just tell him I was tired and left early." Without any other explanation I left. Part way down the street, the music fading, I realized I left Mom's coat in the bathroom and the first flakes of winter were finally swirling down from the dark skies.

Blinded by the hot rush of tears, I kept walking. The snow fell harder and the wind whipped through Jules's shirt like I wasn't wearing anything. I spent a mile trying to convince myself that everything was okay, that I could repair the damage done tonight.

For being such a girl magnet, Jasper knew nothing about girls. Maybe his good looks were really a curse. Because he was able to get girls so easily, he never had to work at it, to really figure out girls out, so that's how he turned into a big fat jerk. And girls kept falling for him.

Which reminded me that Michael was my soul mate and that I'd been right about him all along. But somehow I'd messed that up and now he thought I was easy, and he liked my friend.

When my toes had turned to ice cubes and the snow was clinging in icy clumps to my hair and eyelashes, I broke down and called Zeke. Within minutes he picked me up with a to-go mug of hot cocoa. My heart couldn't help but melt.

He smiled. "You sounded cold."

I broke down all over again after taking the first few sips. "Don't say a word. I don't want to talk about it."

He drove me home and didn't say a word.

In the driveway, I stuttered out a thank you, my voice hoarse and cracking.

Before I could open the car door, he stopped me with a gentle touch of his hand on my arm. With his other hand, he brushed the last of my tears from my chin.

"Hey, it's okay. That's what friends are for, right?"

"Right," I whispered.

CHAPTER 20

THAT NIGHT, MY HOUSE was quiet and still, the silence wrapping around me like one of those blanket/zipper/snuggie things I'd seen on television. Carter was still rocking on at the party and my parents were out to dinner.

The hot water spurted from the tub tap and when it was just scalding enough, I left it to fill the tub. I never take baths, or I haven't since I was a little girl. But after the party and the humiliation and the fact that I couldn't stop shivering, I needed to be completely immersed and forget everything.

In my room, I slipped out of my clothes, remorseful that I hadn't chosen my own clothes for the party, and shrugged on my bathrobe.

The water was practically boiling, and inch by inch I lowered into it. Except, the years had taken their toll.

Instead of it playing out like a movie where there was soft lighting and classical music in the background, I barely fit in the tub and couldn't get my whole body under at the same time. So I rotated. First, my legs were totally under and then I sank down to my chin and my knees poked out. After enough of that, I dried off and put on my yoga pants and hoodie. Complete comfort clothes.

Jasper texted me. *Sorry you left but I took care of everything. You're in. The boy is madly jealous.*

Then another text came through. *Paper due on Monday about theme and symbolism. Pick a classical movie and explain. Three pages. Thanks!*

I stared at my phone, lost in the words of his texts. I knew what to do and I knew what our agreement was but Jasper was so clueless, and in my mind, he had totally screwed up. I'd return the favor.

Furiously, until I couldn't keep my eyes open anymore, I typed out a paper. I shared the document with him, assuming he'd never even read it.

***

MOM SHOOK ME AWAKE the next morning and sat on the edge of my bed. A smile lit her face and she stroked my arm. I mumbled and rolled over.

"Dad told me you had date last night."

I yawned. "The date was great. Better than I imagined."

"How serious is this? Anything a mom should be concerned about?"

With a masked huff, I rolled back over and peered through blurry eyes. "No, it's not that serious. Just a date. And, yes, there might be a second one." Technically, I had a feeling there wouldn't be another date with Jasper but she didn't need to know that. "Can I go back to sleep now?"

She hesitated, probably reining in all outdated dating advice she wanted to give me. "I don't think so." The bed squeaked as she stood. She spoke again from the door. "Jules called and said she'll be here in ten minutes. Something about a shopping trip. So get dressed and come on down."

She'd agreed? Mom was about to feed the machine and encourage my new behavioral pattern with clothes. Maybe I should buy my prom dress now while I had the chance.

The whole way to the store, Jules babbled happily. Once again, we talked about everything except what really mattered. She flitted from one subject to another— prom committee, the Valentine's dance, Zeke and I dressing up. She couldn't stay focused and couldn't stop talking. Kinda like me.

We pulled into the mall and found a spot relatively close to the entrance since it was early. We scurried into the warmth of the shopping plaza and wandered the halls. A few older women walked with their groups in jogging suits and small weights around their wrists.

"Jules?" I asked as she picked her way through sales racks. She's the master at finding great deals. It wasn't that she didn't have the money for full price, but she loved searching for bargains, a natural talent I wished I had. And she knew I couldn't afford full price. "What's this all about?"

She popped up from squinting at a label then squeezed a shirt back on the rack. "Are you kidding me? I heard all about it from Ava who heard from Elena, and— even though I'm so mad you never told me or didn't trust or me whatever—" she grasped my shoulders. "Who cares? This is cause to celebrate."

"Oh, okay. Are you talking about what happened with Jasper?" Not that I wanted to talk about him or even remember last night.

"Yes! Totally!" She studied me, taking in my disheveled appearance. "Hmm. Why don't we start with a coffee?"

"Sounds good."

As we waited in line, she kept the conversation going. "I've hesitated about talking with you about this kind of stuff, because well, you didn't seem very open to it. Anyway, once I heard, I knew we had to talk about it."

We took a seat on high stools at a table for two in the back of the coffee shop. I breathed in the smell of hazelnut.

"I want to know everything." She leaned forward, the gleam of curiosity in her eye.

I sighed. Resigned to the fact that she wanted all the details about my date with Jasper, even though I wanted to forget the whole night. One phrase came to mind. "It was hot." I should've taken that coat off the second I walked through the door, dumb shirt or no.

"Of course, you were with Jasper!" She waved at her face like she was overheated.

"Yeah, well he's totally overrated. I mean I know he's all popular and everything and he's got those dimples but that shouldn't count for everything. That shouldn't make the experience."

Jules stared at me with wide eyes and carefully sipped her skinny latte.

I just kept going, letting my thoughts pour out about the party. "Gosh, I mean halfway through I was a mess and my hair looked like I'd slept on it for a year. I was embarrassed. I know Jasper has a ton of experience in this area, but it's just not for me."

"Really?" Jules squeaked and then couldn't seem to get anything else out.

"I mean I don't think I said one word the whole time. I just wanted to scream in frustration and get out of there."

"I think all girls feel like that. It gets better. I promise."

"I don't think so."

Jules glanced left and right, then leaned over the table and whispered, "I have a book you can borrow. You'll have to hide it from your mom but it explains everything they don't tell you in Health class. Because you shouldn't let one bad experience keep you from trying it again. Maybe Jasper was just wrong for you. Maybe with another guy sex would be better—"

I spit out a mouthful of coffee—and after apologizing profusely and offering a thousand napkins—I thought back over our conversation and last night. "What are you talking about?"

For the first time ever, Jules looked uncomfortable. "What were *you* talking about?"

"The party!"

"You and Jasper didn't...?"

"No. He kissed me once that's it. I left early."

"Oh. That's not what Ava heard..."

The sick feeling of regret washed over my body. I clasped my trembling fingers under the table. That rumor was probably zipping along through every social media known to mankind.

But, that's how rumors get started. All it takes is one lie, one well-meaning lie to get a guy jealous and my reputation is done. What I didn't want to think about was how that conversation got past the two of them. A small voice inside said that Michael must have told Elena, and Elena told Ava, and Ava told Jules. Who else knew? And how could Jasper do that to me?

Understanding passed over her face and she broke down laughing. I laughed too as we recounted all the things I said that she took the wrong way. But inside, a part of me shriveled up, wanting to hide from the truth.

I begged off being tired and Jules drove me home. After pulling into my driveway, I needed to get something off my chest. I wanted to say thanks for wanting to celebrate with me, but when I make a commitment to a guy it's not going to be after a first or a second date. It's going to be when I know I'm in love and when I know it's forever and when I know the guy really cares for me and isn't going to say stupid stuff to his friends.

"When I..." I couldn't finish...because that's when I realized that the guy I just described didn't sound anything like Michael, the one guy I felt sure was destined to be my soul mate.

"Hey, I'll stop by later this week with your costume for Valentine's Day, 'kay?"

"Sure."

Then I was walking into the house and she was driving away.

And I couldn't see through the cloud of confusion that had just fallen over my heart.

CHAPTER 21

I EXPECTED THAT BACK at school, I'd hear and see the whispers, the knowing looks, the rumors. *Little Miss Innocent and rock star God Jasper. They went to a party together. She's easy.* Or maybe even other choice words.

But that's not what happened, and I was positively floored! I stepped out my door in the morning to a clear and cold but bright sunshiny day. The first thing I noticed was a car, sleek and black, purring at the end of my driveway. Jasper waved from the front seat.

This sounds terrible, but I turned around and went back into the house. With my back against the door, I breathed deeply, in and out. Carter slid down the banister and landed on his feet. He studied me and then peered out the window.

"Jasper's here." He said it more like a question.

Mom bustled in with a raisin bran muffin. "Here you go, sweetie." She kissed the top of my forehead, then went back to the kitchen.

Carter was speechless for a moment while everything sank in. Then he whispered, "He's here for you?" He pulled me aside. "Are the rumors true? Because if they are..." His fingers clenched into a fist.

"No!" I hissed out in one frantic breath. "It was one big misunderstanding. Don't do anything." Yeah, sure, I was mad at the guy, but I didn't want my brother beating up on him.

"Are you sure?" he asked, his fingers slowly relaxing.

I nodded emphatically.

A mischievous smile broke out, letting me know he wasn't going to pound Jasper into the ground. He pushed me out the door. "Be careful, today. I'll have your back."

Tentatively, I edged down the icy driveway. Jasper even got out and opened the door for me. "Careful, it's slippery."

I narrowed my eyes. "Thanks." I climbed into the front seat and made sure to slam the door. He probably didn't even realize the damage he'd done.

He got in the driver's seat and reached toward the back. "What kind of coffee do you like?"

"Any kind will do," I said with a layer of frost on my words.

He handed me a to-go cup, filled to the brim with steaming coffee. And it was hazelnut. "Actually, I asked

Jules what you like." He reached back again and came back with a box of donuts. "I ordered a bunch. Jules wasn't sure about this."

"Thanks." I plucked out a strawberry frosted donut with sprinkles. Obviously, he didn't know about my sugar-free diet, and I wasn't about to tell him.

A guy had never gone out of their way like this for me. I peeked at Jasper, who pulled onto the road. The early sunshine slanted through the window, highlighting the light scruff on his chin. I wondered if—after he ruined everything with his big mouth—I'd still get the floaty feeling, the one I got when around him and when he turned his eyes on me. Not that I had a crush on him, but it was Jasper. He took me to a party. He picked me up for school. Okay, fine, we had a deal but no one knew that. I gulped at the thought of the paper.

He leaned over to kiss me on the cheek at a stop sign. "You were pretty speedy with the paper. Thanks."

I couldn't eat the donut or accept his gifts until I set the ground rules. I couldn't be too furious with him, because it was partly my fault for being so vague, assuming Jasper wouldn't royally screw it up. "No more lies to Michael or anyone else about anything we've done in the kissing department, especially when it's not true. Got it?"

He flashed me a sideways glance. "Yeah, sorry about that. It didn't go as planned."

I held back an annoyed grunt. Guys can be so clueless. I'd thought about breaking up with him, but then how would that make me look? Even worse! So I had to ride this scheme out and repair my reputation.

After a closer look at his face, I noticed a yellow and purple bruise around his eye and the fact that he wore make-up. I almost coughed donut over the dashboard of his spaceship and that wouldn't have been good.

"What happened to your eye?" I asked, picking at the rim of my coffee.

He gently touched it with his fingers and grimaced. "At the party, I slipped on the steps and landed on the corner of a bench seat after talking to your guy." He winked. "But anything for you, darling."

I decided not to mention the make-up and that it was the wrong color for his skin tone. Even I could see that, and I wasn't a make-up expert. I also didn't mention my real thoughts. Jasper was a gifted athlete—what were the odds he'd trip?

From the bathroom, I'd heard Michael's tone of voice. What if Michael punched him a good one—for my honor? That's something a soul mate would do. But even with that thought to console me, the gnawing doubt remained.

Jasper smiled the whole way to and into school. And why not? He thought he was going to ace a paper for the first time in his life. Maybe.... Regret started creeping in and I had second thoughts about writing his paper when I was emotional and tired. I possibly should've waited until morning to read it over a second time.

This charade didn't end there. He walked me through the halls, his arm draped over my shoulder. He stayed with me until just before the bell rang and he was waiting for me as soon as I stepped outside the classroom. By fourth period, I was wondering how these girls did it all the time.

My cheek muscles were sore from smiling at everyone who talked to me, and at Jasper who flashed a constant smile, probably so his dimples would work their magic on me. Before lunch, I'd had it. I pushed into the bathroom and slumped down on a toilet, exhausted and drained of all energy.

"Love bug?" He knocked on the door to the bathroom. "Elena said you were in here."

Ugh. Love bug? I wanted to puke, but I mustered up the pep to respond. "Yup! Be right out." I looked in the mirror, but all I noticed was the blank, lost expression reflected in my eyes. I whispered, "Remember why you're doing this, Cassidy. Remember your goals. Remember Michael. Remember prom."

When I stepped outside into Jasper's clutches, I didn't feel any better. I had to cling to the hope that my plan was working. Outside the cafeteria, Jasper paused and whispered, "This is it, babe. Show time."

We strolled into the cafeteria, Jasper acting like one-half of the super couple, me feeling like the second half of a losing football game. This was my Hail Mary, but something told me I'd already lost.

The social spotlights were on us and it felt like we were striding in slow motion. I should've been flipping my hair back and smiling, like this wasn't just part of a plan. Instead, I focused on placing one foot in front of the other and not looking anyone in the eye. He led me right to his table with Jules, Carter, Ava, Elena, and...Michael. I peeked around for Zeke but couldn't find him.

Michael nodded, a cool look on his face, but one I was getting used to. Gone were the days when I got even one real smile from him, but at least he acknowledged me.

I forced a smile. "Hi, everyone."

Jasper squeezed my hand and after he sat, he patted the seat neat to him. I should have felt honored and proud for this spot, but instead I felt a little bit like a dog about to be fed a treat for good behavior. I hoped to make it through lunch without saying a word, the invisible person, who people talk around. No such luck.

"How did you get home from the party?" Elena asked, her voice pointed and sharp, no pretenses.

"I walked. It was a nice night out." I flashed back to how Zeke's hand on my arm felt and the concern on his face and in his words.

"It started blizzarding," Ava said flatly. "We almost couldn't leave the party."

"Right. There was that." My cheeks filled with heat and I launched into a typical speech, feeling the heat grow stronger with every word. "But ever since I was little I've loved the snow and the cold. There are lots of tricks to staying warm in a blizzard. I just think of the hottest, steamiest day of summer when the heat is so unbearable that you'd do anything for a nice cold snowfall." I shrugged. "And that's what gets me through. Of course, wearing a warm coat is of the most importance—"

Carter shot up from the table. "Hey, sis. I forgot that Mom wanted you to call her." He put his hands on my shoulder and practically dragged me from the table. "We'll see all of you later."

We were walking out and the lunchroom faded into black behind us. He led us outside into the crisp air, fresh white snow on the ground. I leaned over, breathing hard. "Thank you!"

"You know what they're all saying, don't you?" he asked, showing absolutely no sympathy.

"I have an idea."

"You've got to set them straight." He pushed me up. "Enough with the fake panic attacks. Get over it."

I gasped, choking at the cold air in my lungs. "I'm not faking it. That was horrible. How can you handle all that pressure?"

"Well, first, I don't act like an idiot and say stupid things. I don't hook up with the most popular guy and then walk around like his little toy all day."

Okay, that hurt. First, because my own brother believed I'd even want to work my way up the popular pole. Second, he had no room to talk.

"No, you just play Taylor Swift music and upload your music videos to YouTube to get dates, instead of just being a nice guy." I was on a role and there was no stopping me as the anger spiraled out of control. "You worked hard to get in with that group." I ignored his shocked expression. "Yeah, that's right. You can pretend all you want that it's about being the fun, flirty guy who likes to date, but I can see how over the months you slowly wiggled your way into the group. So don't you dare say anything about me."

As I continued to yell at Carter, the door to the building opened and someone walked out, just as I was building to a crescendo.

"And I can do whatever I want with a guy!" I yelled. "Even if it is Jasper."

Zeke stood a couple feet behind us, his sneakers buried in the snow, his face pale, but he recovered and wore a mask of indifference.

"You go for it then." Carter flipped around and pushed Zeke back a few steps, leaving the two of us in awkward silence.

"Uh, that's not what it sounded like." I peeked at Zeke, who wouldn't look at me. How would I even begin to explain the truth? I'd need more than a few minutes. "Just a sibling fight. You know...."

He held up his hands, palms out. "No need to explain anything. Didn't mean to interrupt. Just wanted to let you know that Jules wants us to go shopping this afternoon for prom decorations because there's a sale. And Ava's coming too." He turned and went inside.

I wanted to scream. I wanted to drop to my knees and beg Zeke to believe the truth, that Jasper just kissed me. That's it. But my mouth wouldn't move, and the words died in my throat. Zeke was my friend, and for some reason, I cared about what he thought.

***

As INSTRUCTED, I MET Zeke and Ava after school. We piled into Ava's car and zipped over to the friendly mega store. I automatically took the back, especially after Ava glared at me and then sweetly invited Zeke to sit in the front seat. She was in all out peacock-mode. I know it's the male bird that flaunts and struts, but there was no better word for what she was doing—it was kinda embarrassing.

She talked and giggled and tilted her head at all the right times and talked some more and flirted like she was in a marathon. Zeke took it all in, not gushing and not acting all stupid like I did around Jasper or Michael. With every cool response he gave, Ava's instinct to show off her feminine wiles increased. I sat in the back and gagged with every sugary comment.

In the store, I split the list and wandered off by myself, gathering the items. Once I was done, I left the cart up at the front and trudged through the store to find them. The falsetto giggle couldn't be missed, except instead of turning the corner and letting them know I was there, I stood behind the display of candy Valentine hearts and listened.

Ava was gushing. "Why I'd love to go to the Valentine Dance with you. I thought you'd never ask!"

"Um..."

I never heard Zeke's response, because I wobbled and sank against the display. Why did that bother me so much? Did I like Zeke as more than a good friend? My sensibilities were overwhelmed, and apparently, so wasn't the display, because it crashed to the ground, boxes scattering everywhere.

"Cassidy?" Ava said it like, of course, who else would knock over a candy display in a store.

Zeke didn't even look at me.

CHAPTER 22

THE REST OF THE week went pretty much the same. Jasper coddled me like I was a toddler, incapable of walking to class or making decisions for myself. Every day at lunch he patted the seat next to him. Any lingering floaty feelings for the guy had completely popped and faded into nothing, especially now that his perfect veneer had cracked and I knew him better.

Like, for example, his breath doesn't smell so hot after lunch. Or the fact that, by the end of the day, his cologne has faded, leaving behind a normal guy smell, which isn't always good. Or that when he's exaggerating or telling a half-truth, he punctuates the end of the sentence with his classic smile as if to convince himself and others that everything is as perfect as it seems.

Each time I mentioned ending our deal to Jasper, because this whole popular thing was exhausting and I wasn't even sure how well the plan was working, he convinced me to give it until the Valentine's dance. In other words, he had a couple more papers he wanted me to write.

My gut feeling said to run, but what if he was right? What if all it took was for Michael to witness Jasper and I in each other's arms? I couldn't give up now.

Friday dawned and I'd never looked worse. I'm not even sure an injection of coffee straight into my veins would've helped. I was barely out of the shower when Jules stopped by to pick me up. I'd tried to forget about the whole dress-up-in-a-costume idea because I didn't feel like a princess. I didn't feel beautiful or worthy to wear a crown—even if it was made of plastic. And the jewels would probably fall off by third period.

On the drive back to her house, Jules chatted on about the plan for the day, completely peppy and enthusiastic...until she wasn't. "We've run into a few complications, but there shouldn't be a problem."

"Like what?"

"Just a few costume glitches but nothing we can't take care of." She laughed and waved her hand. Totally fake.

"What else?" Because I could tell there was more.

"Well, after much consideration, Ava and I decided that with the splash you and Jasper have made on the social scene that it really should be Jasper dressed up as your prince today, not Zeke. I mean, it just makes sense, right?"

"Right." But the word barely made it out because I'd been looking forward to the break from Jasper.

"You two are going to the dance together, you're a couple now. We have to give the crowds what they want."

I had a feeling Ava had more to do with this decision than Jules. Zeke had popped up on her radar and for some reason, she didn't want anyone else near him. What I couldn't figure out was what had changed. Maybe she noticed that he's a caring, loyal friend who is always there. Maybe she noticed the way he's not uber hot-looking like Jasper but cute in his own way especially when he smiles. Maybe she noticed his lip ring and crooked teeth and found it just as cute and endearing as I did. Maybe.

Maybe I should've noticed all that sooner.

***

JASPER WALTZED OUT OF the bathroom, dressed in clothes, not in the costume. "I don't think so."

He flashed his typical lazy smile, which I've since learned is the smile he gives in every situation, even if he's not happy at all. Like now. His muscles were all flexed and tense and his hair was a little mussed for this early in the morning.

"Come on, Jasper. We need you. This is perfect." She nudged me and whispered, "Go work your magic. He's your boyfriend." She shoved me forward.

She probably wanted me to slather on the charm and use words like honey pie or sweetums. Not happening. I swayed forward but probably looked more off balance than sexy. "Aren't we going to be prince and princess today?"

His smile faded and he twirled a lock of my hair around his finger. "You know I'd do just about anything for you, Pumpkin." He leaned forward, letting his lips graze my cheek, whispering. "Especially since you write such fantastic papers,"—he spoke louder—"but there's no way I'm wearing that. Sorry."

He kissed me on the cheek. "See you at school." Then he left.

Jules crumpled. "I'm sorry about the costume. I really am. It's just that our fundraising didn't make enough to cover the costs of what we wanted. This was the best I could do and now the whole day will be shot because all our plans revolved around you two in costumes. Everyone's looking forward to it."

It's funny how the life-changing moments come without any warning, like a bolt of lightning flashing across the hot summer sky. Last year or last month I'd never do what I was about to do, but I'd changed.

I was still changing. This week had taught me something about the popular crowd. I used to think it was about the looks and the clothes but it's more than that. It's about perception. Creating the mirage that someone has what others want, whether it's a car, a fancy house, nice clothes or the hot guy...or confidence.

For this past week, I'd jumped the social totem pole because of Jasper and my supposed sleep patterns with him. But the view from the top was no brilliant, mountaintop sunset. If anything, looking down, I could see the muddy tracks and destruction I'd left behind. The huge garbage pile underneath me, the horrid smell wafting up into the air. I didn't like the view or the smell from the top.

"I'll do it anyway. And I'll speak alone at lunchtime too."

Jules perked up. Her face went from surprise to something deeper. If I was changing and learning, so was my cousin. "Why would you do that? Especially...after last summer?" Her last three words came out as a whisper.

I shrugged, fighting back the tears. I knew Jules was sorry. Eventually, we'd talk about it. Until then, I forgave her. I just wanted my cousin and best friend back. "Because I said I would."

***

I STOOD OUTSIDE THE school, hesitant and doubting. There are many perks to wearing a giant, puffy red heart costume that made me three sizes larger than I was and crinkled whenever I moved.

One, everyone would have to clear out of the way in hall, so no being late to class. Two, I'd have fun accidentally knocking papers off desks. Three, the material was really soft and velvety, very comforting. Four, I'd have fun memories to share with grandkids someday. Five, well, I'd be the envy of every girl in school—obviously.

Of course, just being my luck, the first person I bumped into at school was Michael. He laughed, then controlled it, finally speaking in a normal voice. "Cassidy?"

I stopped, wishing to God I was wearing something else. I felt like he hadn't talked to me in days, other than brief hellos in the hall and nods in the cafeteria.

"Why are you doing this?" He focused on me as if trying to solve some kind of computer program, and that if he thought about it long enough, he'd find the answer.

I sighed. "For Jules. I wasn't supposed to do it alone…but…oh, never mind. Long story."

My locker wasn't far away and the clock was ticking, so I made my down the hall. Michael followed. I grabbed my binder and a couple books.

He leaned against my locker and pushed his glasses up farther on his nose. "I don't get it. Why?"

"You know Jules when she gets an idea in her head. The tiny hearts on my cheeks were a last minute flash of brilliance and the tiara was the princess touch, because really I was supposed to be a princess and Jasper was supposed to be my—"

"That's really nice of you." He coughed and his cheeks turned a little pink. He stumbled over his words and restarted a couple times before finally spitting it out. "Last summer, I really wanted this scholarship to go to a science camp. I mean I wanted it so bad I was obsessed. I went to extremes. I more embarrassed myself than anything…"

Was he about to admit he liked me? That Elena was the science camp he really wanted and how he realized a little late that the extremes he had to go to weren't worth it in the long run. No way. I waited for my heart to soar and my stomach to flip-flop, but nothing happened. "Don't worry about it. I know this is extreme, but she's my cousin."

"She's lucky to have you for a friend." He flashed me a warm smile, one I hadn't seen since last summer.

I leaned against my locker, absorbing our conversation. Wow. That was totally unexpected. In a good way.

For the next couple hours, I delivered all the carnations. I just took one and put my name on it. Jules doesn't need more than ten and I figured she owed me.

Jasper was supposed to be with me but I sucked it up and floated from class to class on the knowledge that Michael was finally starting to steer in my direction. Maybe my whole jealousy plan had worked. I could tell him later that I never did anything with Jasper and that I was saving myself for true love.

A bit tired, feet hurting, I arrived at English class a couple minutes past the bell but all I had to do was wiggle my hips to cause a little crinkle action and the teacher nodded me on to my desk.

"Excuse me. Pardon me." I pushed my way down the narrow alley between the rows of desks until I reached an empty desk in the back.

Zeke raised an eyebrow, and I shrugged. He pointed to Jasper and raised his hands in question. I shrugged again. It's really hard to sign or mouth the words: my fake boyfriend is so vain he didn't want to dress up in a big fat puffy heart costume even if he could wear a crown.

Mr. Troller stood at the front of the room, fidgeting by straightening his bow tie several times. Finally, when my crinkles stopped, he cleared his throat.

"I don't need to tell you that it's your senior year. You're about to leave the nest and fly into the world. You'll have to find jobs and complete work or you won't have a job for long. Consider your homework assignments as practice for the real world." He paused, searching the faces of his students.

Some students groaned and hid their faces in their hands. Others looked pretty nonchalant as if they could drop off to sleep any moment. Then there were the top students, confident of their work and their ability to follow directions. Today, Jasper fell into that category.

Hot needle pricks of panic spread all over. The puffy costume didn't help as the temperature in the room skyrocketed. I flashed back to the night after the party, when I was hurt and so low that nothing mattered. I whipped off his assignment, not thinking about the consequences.

Mr. Troller continued his little speech as he passed out the papers. I watched as Jasper's floated and landed. Was that a big, fat F? Of course it was. I slumped low in my seat, keeping an eye on him.

He looked at the paper and once the grade had registered, he folded it once and slipped it into his backpack. Kind of like this morning, when he was more than angry that we suggested he wear such a ridiculous costume. He was boiling and bubbling on the inside, but to everyone else he was cool and in control with that lazy smile of his that said everything was okay in the world.

Mr. Troller lectured on theme and symbolism and I hung my head in shame. Zeke excused himself part way through, and I almost begged him to take me with him, anything to escape what could be my ultimate doom.

Finally, the bell rang, and for a stuffed heart, I moved pretty fast out of the room and into the safety of the hall. But it was impossible to hide. Minutes later, Jasper was right next to me, his arm draped on my shoulder, walking with me, step for step, and not saying a word.

Yeah, I was pretty much dead.

***

I THOUGHT MY LIFE was over, but Jasper kept all his rage hidden inside. I could tell by the way he walked, how tightly he held my hand, and the scowl when he thought no one was looking. He might have had everyone else fooled, but not me.

As usual, Jasper patted the seat next to him at the table. Underlying his smile, his face was pale, and a coldness had settled in his eyes. If I wasn't so hot, I would've shivered under his glare. The girls flashed their jealous looks as they picked at their lunches and I didn't eat anything.

"You nervous?" Jasper whispered.

He must have been listening to Mr. Troller the day he talked about hiding meanings in our papers that only some readers would get. In this case, I was the reader and I knew exactly what he meant. So, of course, I babbled.

"Well, I am dressed as a heart, *the only one dressed as a heart*, so a part of me has been on edge all day. This is nothing like wearing a puffy scarf with bright colors. Jules can get away with that but for some reason I can't wear scarves. They make me nervous, so yeah, you could say I'm a bit nervous, and then there's the pop quiz I heard we might be having in math—"

Jules tapped me on the shoulder. "You're up."

"Now?" I squeaked.

She pulled me aside, biting her lip, and squeezing my hand. "Listen, I'm so grateful. I've been thinking. You don't have to do this for me. I know the speech is a little corny." She fell silent for a moment. When she looked back up, she was blinking back tears. "You've already done enough."

Somehow I think she was talking about more than just today.

I glanced past her at Jasper with his cocky smile. I couldn't believe I once thought he was cute. I couldn't believe I thought he could get away with rolling up his khakis and wearing moccasins, because he so couldn't. I couldn't believe I swooned over him in the bathroom. It was like he felt my stare as he turned his head and winked at me. There were a thousand words in that one wink, and I didn't like any of them.

"No." I cut Jules off. "I'll do it. I said I would, and I will because that's the kind of person I am."

"Okay. I'll owe you one." She handed me my script and backed off to find a seat.

Across the cafeteria, Jules had set up a small stage with a microphone. I looked at the blurred words on the page, then strode across the room, followed by whispers and laughter.

I tapped the microphone. "Testing!" It squeaked and then my voice came through, booming. All the students cringed. "Oops. Sorry."

I studied all my classmates, while trying to muster up some spit so I could talk. Some I'd known since elementary school, some I'd befriended in the past couple years, and others I barely knew. But we all had something in common. We were all seniors, and we all wanted this to be a memorable year. That was it. I knew what to say even though it was nothing like the script Jules had written for me, because without a prince, it wouldn't work even though she'd crossed out some lines and written in other ones.

I leaned into the microphone. "You might be wondering why I'm wearing this big puffy heart costume. To tell you the truth, I am too." I took a few moments and breathed in, clearing away all the distractions. "This wasn't what was planned. I wasn't supposed to be the only one dressed like this. In fact, I wasn't supposed to be a heart at all. I was supposed to be a beautiful princess."

Several boys scoffed and muttered comments. I ignored them.

"But fate has a way of stepping in. And sometimes deep down, we don't want to be princesses but we want to be a heart, filled with blood pumping through our arteries and veins. We want to be alive. Without our hearts we'd be nothing, just zombies walking through the halls..."

I lost my train of thought and had the feeling I was messing this up and mixing metaphors. I was losing my audience. Many of them had gone back to eating and chatting with their neighbors. Jules waves frantically from the back and pointed to the sheet of paper.

Feeling a little dizzy and wanting the floor to crack open and swallow me, I lifted the paper and started reading. Something about needing my prince when the cafeteria door crashed open and I heard the strums of a guitar.

A collective gasp came from everyone, and I almost cried when Carter walked through the door with his guitar hanging off his shoulder by a strap. He was strumming and humming and everyone was enthralled. But most importantly, their eyes were off me.

He shuffled over and stood next to me. I moved the microphone over. He started singing a Taylor Swift song, and I almost laughed and cried at the same time. But then everyone pointed.

I peered around Carter, who kept singing, at Zeke who pushed his way through the narrow doorway, with a crinkle and a bit of a red face. His red heart billowed around him in puffs of red and velvet and a trail of glitter. A crown sat on top of his head—my prince.

I blinked and blinked, and my throat got so choked up I couldn't say a thing, which is unusual for me, as Zeke waddled over. Is that what I'd looked like all day?

He held out his hand. "Would the princess like this dance?"

I couldn't say a word, just nodded. He led me over to the side and put his arm around me and held my other hand, as sweaty as it was, in the waltz position. Our puffy bellies bumped into each other, knocking off even more glitter.

He smiled, oblivious to the open-mouthed stares we were getting. "Just follow my lead."

In the next few moments, while Carter's husky voice quieted the crowds, Zeke twirled me around and we danced as only two hearts could, side by side. It was the most romantic and embarrassing thing I'd ever done.

"Don't worry about what anyone thinks. You look great," he whispered, as if he could read my thoughts. "Would you go to the Valentine's dance with me?"

What? I stumbled out a few words.

"I know it's late. I should've asked earlier."

All I could manage was one word. "Ava."

He huffed. "Ava?"

"That day. In store." Why couldn't I speak in full sentences?

"Oh, right. I never asked her. She took something I said and jumped on it. So..."

I wanted to say yes, but as the guitar got louder and approached the final chorus, kids started singing, so we could no longer whisper. At the end, when Zeke dipped me low to the tiled floor, everyone stood and clapped and cheered.

I had a real date to the dance.

I just had to say yes.

CHAPTER 23

I DON'T THINK I'LL ever understand guys and how their brains work. It's a mystery and one I hope to grasp by the time I'm eighty with white hair and my teeth falling out. Here's what would happen in normal situations: girl pisses off her kinda-sorta-boyfriend and kinda-sorta-boyfriend breaks up with the girl.

In real life. In normal situations that's what should happen. There have to be some scientific laws out there about push and pull or action and reaction that would verify this.

I fully expected, in fact was a little relieved, that Jasper would be breaking off his kinda-sorta-relationship with me. He'd brush me off like cookie crumbs on his favorite shirt, and I could go back to my quiet existence.

Except that's not what happened. That afternoon in the cafeteria on the day of the Valentine's Dance, after

Carter finished his song, after the two puffy hearts finished their awkward dance, and after the crowds finished cheering, Jasper strode to the front of the microphone, or more like grabbed it from Carter.

With a lazy grin to charm the crowds, he used his official I'm-the-popular-one-here-and-don't-forget-it voice and officially asked me to the Valentine's dance. Everyone oohed and sighed and well, what was I supposed to say?

For a brief second, which felt like an eternity with my past, present, and future all tied up in this moment, I looked between Zeke and Jasper.

Jasper held his arms out to me while the crowds started clapping in rhythm. Now, I'll admit I was the one who got myself in this situation to make Michael jealous. But I'm not sure that had worked at all up to this point, as he was currently hanging all over Elena, probably relieved it wasn't him up there with me.

Zeke knew me. He knew I rambled when I was nervous. He knew I was horrified about walking around like a poofy heart all day. He knew what I needed and when, and I'd been pushing him away all year.

Jasper leaned toward me. "This isn't optional."

That was all he had to say. I'd better play along with his little act, or my academic and social act would be over. I wanted to say no to Jasper and go to the dance with Zeke, but I didn't really have a choice.

Zeke knew the moment I made the decision to go with Jasper, because in one expression he told me goodbye. He stepped away and faded into the crowds, despite being dressed like a big red internal organ.

I stumbled into Jasper's arms. He stroked my velvety back and whispered, "That's my girl."

Ugh.

***

I WORE THE SAME black dress to the Valentine's Dance that I wore to the Christmas one. I mean it's not like anyone really saw me for very long, and it's a black dress. No one would remember. Except maybe Ava, but she didn't care anymore. She had Zeke.

I could go into the details about the dance. For example, how Jasper kept me by his side the whole time except barely talked to me. He laughed with his friends, joked with classmates, and I stood there like a complete doofus. I think for the first time in my life, I wondered if I'd used up all my words. Because I had nothing to say.

Oh, Jasper was the model date. He brought me a bouquet of obnoxious flowers. I guess with him, the bigger the better. He played romantic music in the car as we drove to the dance. He made sure to dance with me almost every slow song with his cheek pressed up against mine.

I guess in a way I deserved it. When I scheme or anything close to it, it comes back to haunt me. Last spring? I ended up in the Program.

Steal a dress from someone who didn't need it? Spend the Christmas dance alone, scared and in the dark of a science lab wearing a teacher's smelly lab coat.

Make your kinda-sorta-boyfriend look like he's second best or not man enough to dress up in a stupid costume? End up glued to his side being showered with all sorts of false attention when all I wanted was to dance with someone else.

I got one moment to myself and was about to enjoy a cool, refreshing root beer, when Michael approached me, shifting back and forth on his feet.

"Can we talk?" he asked.

"Sure. About what?" I couldn't help it. My heart fluttered just a tiny bit. This was the second time in one day he was talking to me. Sadly, the fluttering had more to do with my long history of thinking I loved him. I was pretty sure those days were gone.

"I think you got the wrong impression earlier at school."

"What do you mean?" I sighed, feeling the exhaustion of the whole Valentine's thing. The holiday should be outlawed due to the unnecessary stress and strain it brings to the unattached.

He stammered a bit, and pink heightened in his cheeks even in the dimmed lighting.

"Spit it out." I encouraged.

"Well, when I was talking about the science camp and getting in and going to extremes, I think you misunderstood me."

"I know." I patted him on the shoulder. "You've been going to extremes all year to catch Elena's eye, and you finally realized that you're done jumping through hoops."

He cleared his throat and straightened up. "That's just it. That's not what I was talking about. I was talking about you."

I leaned forward and batted my eyes. My heart quickened. Was he about to say that he really wanted me?

He grabbed my hand. "I'm concerned about you."

"Huh?" His hand was growing a bit sweaty.

"I mean there are dangers to, well, to fighting a dragon..." he glanced at Jasper "...without wearing armor or to sleeping without your shield by your side. Know what I mean?"

"Um, yeah, I guess so." Totally didn't get it.

He sighed and acted a bit flustered that I wasn't catching on. "I'd hate to see you wind up with an open sword wound, all alone." When I flashed him another confused look, he lowered his voice. "If you dressed up like a heart for Jasper, not saying you did, but if that's the case...he's not worth it. You should like someone who appreciates you and treats you the way you deserve to be treated. Not him, but someone else."

"Ohhh." I got it and my face felt like a volcano had exploded in my head—or I should say a dragon breathed fire on me. In other words, my plan to make him jealous completely failed.

He nudged my cheek with his knuckles in a move you'd pull with your kid sister. "So, we're cool?"

"Definitely. Totally. We're way more than cool. We're like in the Arctic surrounded by icebergs, slowly going numb, hidden under so many layers of ice that it would take days to chip us out. Of course, that might be a little too much because we wouldn't want to get hypothermia or lose any limbs from frost bite…"

He flashed a weak smile. "Great. I'll see you around." He turned back, probably to find Elena.

"You bet," I said, even though he didn't hear me, then turned and walked back to Jasper.

That's how the Valentine's dance went—another milestone memory for me during my senior year, the pinnacle of my life. The drive home was another matter entirely.

Over the soft romantic music, Jasper laid it all out. He finally reacted to my writing his paper on the wrong subject and getting him a big, fat F. I hate those red pens.

He pulled into my driveway and grasped my hand. He turned his lazy grin on me. "I know you were just joking with me by writing that paper. But I'm going to give you a chance to make it up." He stroked the top of my hand with his thumb. "For the rest of the year, you can write all my

English essays...and I'll be sure to read all of them. This way, your dear Michael will never know of your plans to make him jealous, and the school won't find out you've been cheating."

I stared out the front window, zoning out. I didn't want Michael anymore, which meant I didn't need Jasper anymore. "I'm breaking up with you."

Jasper made this shocked, offended noise. "What?"

"I'm breaking up with you. You're dumped."

His face bloomed into a fiery red. "I don't think so. After that stunt you pulled with my paper?"

I laughed. "You know, red isn't really your color." I patted his cheek. "I'll write your papers, for now. But our relationship is finished." I sighed. "I just don't love you anymore."

On that note, I was about to climb out of the car, when he placed his hand on my leg. "Sorry. I'm not ready to lose you. The charade will continue a while longer, or your academic career will be..." He ran his finger across his neck. Then he chuckled. "Anyway, I like you. You've got spunk. I'll see you in school." Then after a quick kiss, he said, "And you're kinda cute."

I left and went inside, with definitely no floaty, bubbly feeling.

After showering and slipping into my most comfy jammies, I crawled into bed. In the dark, in a place where I could be honest and no one could judge, I thought back on the dance. I thought about what I'd ignored all night.

The image of Zeke dancing with Ava, and the way she draped her arms around his neck and nibbled on his lip ring. He was responding and talking and laughing and whispering with a girl...that wasn't me.

CHAPTER 24

THE MONDAY AFTER THE dance, I begged Jules to pull me from the prom decoration committee. I couldn't handle the mushy gushy in-my-face behavior with Zeke that Ava flaunted whenever I happened to be around. I handed the whole medieval theme over to them. My one fleeting addition was digging out Carter's Halloween costume from middle school. He'd spent days making chain mail and the best fake-looking armor out there. It even came with a wicked-looking sword—plastic, of course.

And then I told Mr. G. that I was done with the support group. I'd had enough support.

The week after the dance, Carter and I went downtown. I bought a cup of hot chocolate and found a seat on a bench lining Main Street. It was February, and the bitter chill of winter had definitely set in, but today, the sun had made the sky bright and clear.

Carter slid onto the bench next to me. "Hey."

I looked at him, at his bright eyes, shining with enthusiasm and humor. He wore regular clothes, but somehow was a hot market. "How do you do it?"

"Do what?"

"Get all the girls. We're not so different, you and I." After all, we were twins.

"Now, that's where you're wrong." He stood and held out his hand to me.

I didn't take it. He wasn't getting out of this conversation with simple distractions. "What do you mean by that?"

He sat back down with a huff. "You and I are very different. You believe in true love and all that kind of stuff." He waved his hands. "I believe in the power of perception and creating a truth that other people want."

His words didn't sit right with me, and I was about ready to walk off and leave him with his next hair-brained scheme. "You mean lying?"

Carter grabbed his chest above his heart and gasped. Then he smirked and quit the dramatics. "No, I don't mean lying. That's the last way to get someone to like you. No offense, sis."

"None taken." But it was true. And I was tired of it.

"I just see what would fit with me and what I like to do and how others will interpret that. You want to see my next scheme in action?"

"Oh, no."

He smiled, a glint in his eye. "Come on. Watch a master in action."

With great suspicion, I stood. "I guess so."

As we walked down the sidewalk of Main Street, I felt like every car that drove by, every classmate that waved, knew we were up to something—even though I didn't even know what.

"For example, your little Valentine's Day stunt was terrific."

"Stunt?" Obviously he didn't know his twin well, because that day was going down as the most humiliating day of my life! Someday, when I have to share in a college class or on the job about my experiences, I'll be too embarrassed to even share that one.

"Uh, yeah. Wished I'd thought of it."

"What?" Another car beeped and the kids inside waved. I waved back, clueless as to who they were.

"You did something that no one else dared to do and then the top jock, the most wanted guy in school, said it was okay when he asked you to the dance."

I snorted. "Clearly they didn't understand what was really going on then."

"I don't even want to know the details, but even your flat-out rejection of Zeke-Man, created a wave of empathy. Now the girls are hot for him, even Ava."

"Ava was already interested."

"Well, now she's full out, gung ho for the guy."

And that explained it. Why Ava's interest in Zeke had turned into a full-blown obsession. Why all of a sudden she wanted the guy that wasn't the best looking in school, or the top athlete, or on the path to make millions. And it was all my doing. I might as well have pushed her straight into his arms. I'd never forget the flash of betrayal in his eyes when I chose Jasper.

I must've scowled or showed my extreme dislike about Ava, because Carter picked up on it right away and called me on it.

"Do you like Zeke?" He opened the door of a shop, the bell jangling at the top. I embraced the sudden rush of warm air.

My heart ached. I didn't care where we were. I couldn't hold it inside anymore. All it took was Carter saying the words out loud. Hot tears spilled down my cheeks. My chest heaved and strange hiccup noises escaped my mouth. I blubbered while Carter escorted me back out into the cold air and to the side of the shop.

He hugged me for a minute or so, then pulled away. "Is this about Zeke? Spill it."

I didn't even know where to begin. After a few more heaves, I took a few deep breaths. Between hiccups, I told him that I'd made a deal with Jasper to make Michael jealous and that Jasper and I weren't really dating. That, in exchange, I'd promised to write his papers. Except, after the party I was mad and wrote an essay on the wrong topic. My plan failed. Michael didn't like me. I'd lost Zeke.

And Jasper was still forcing me to write his papers or he'd tell.

Carter pulled me into his arms and gave me another brother/sister hug. "Wow. So I guess you like Zeke."

"Yes." I laughed/sobbed. I'd just realized it too late.

"You need cheering up. I know just the thing." He pulled away and wiped my tears with his sleeve.

Even though my situation hadn't changed, I felt lighter.

He hooked his arm in mine and led me back into the store. "Watch and learn, sis."

I wrinkled my nose at the familiar pet store smell—not my favorite. Carter went up to the front desk and immediately got into an in-depth conversation filled with head nods and questions and more head nods and more questions. The clerk scribbled something down on a piece of paper and then we were on our way out the door.

"What was that all about?"

"You'll see. I'm going to need your help."

On the car ride to wherever we were going, I thought about Zeke and how he wanted to be my friend through out the Program. He'd always wanted to be my friend. He never seemed to mind the crazy. I let out a little sigh. I'd been too obsessed with Michael and couldn't let go of goals I'd thought about for far too long.

Carter brought me to a farm on the outskirts of town. The owners had a new litter of puppies and were giving away the golden/lab mix for practically nothing.

"You're going to use innocent puppies?" I asked, faking shock.

"Yup."

I totally fell for it. The golden fluffy ball of fur melted my heart, and I finally agreed with Carter that I might be wrong about fish.

Even Mom and Dad, who swore up and down that we'd never have a dog, wavered when the puppy fell on its stomach and pouted as if it knew Mom and Dad held his life in their hands. But when Carter mentioned his name was Hemingway, after Mom's favorite author, she relented.

I held the little guy and scratched behind his ears. "I know. I know you don't like the name anymore than I do." That's when I realized the small things Carter does to win people over, like naming his dog after a person someone else loves. A strategy I highly doubted would ever work for me.

The very next day, Carter started his new series of YouTube videos, titled Me and My Dog. What no one knows though, is that even after Carter cajoled and offered treats, every night, the puppy sneaked into my room and curled up on the foot of my bed.

From there on out we were like a movie. Hemingway became part of my routine. I talked to him in the early hours of the morning when the sun was barely making a dent on the winter cold and he was making yellow spots in the snow. I told him my problems, my frustrations at Jasper and how his head was getting so big from all the As he was getting on his essays that it was about explode.

Hemingway liked that one. I could tell by the way he jumped up on me—or it could have been cookie crumbs from my midnight snack the night before.

Sometimes, after we came inside to eat breakfast, over hot cocoa, while the house was still, I'd whisper that I'd been crazy to dream of being with Michael and going to prom with him anyway.

CHAPTER 25

MARCH AND APRIL WENT by pretty fast. I was busy trying to avoid Zeke and Ava and trying not to gag at Michael, who was still gaga over Elena. Even though I was trying to move on, it still bothered me. Plus, I was writing all my essays for English and Jasper's too. I was in a rut and wished for a little bit of Carter's magic as far as ideas to change how people perceived me, because, according to my brother, that was my problem.

A breakthrough came when Aunt Lulu showed up at our door one bright, early Saturday morning. I'd already taken Hem for a walk and was on my second mug of hot chocolate.

She didn't even need to enter the house, but from the doorway, in her booming but ladylike voice, announced she was taking me for breakfast. At least there would be food involved.

Aunt Lulu isn't much of an animal person and if she'd given me warning, I would've made sure Hemingway was up in my room, but he turned the corner of the kitchen island and scampered over to meet her.

She screeched while I pulled Hemingway away to calm him down and tell him not to take it personally and that Aunt Lulu was really just deathly allergic to dogs. Obediently, Hemingway padded back upstairs.

"Is that thing yours?" Aunt Lulu pulled herself straight and asked with much indignation.

Thankfully, I didn't have to lie. "He's Carter's and his name is Hemingway."

"Hmpf. That boy."

That's all that was said. It didn't take me long to get ready. I threw on a different shirt and applied bubblegum lip gloss. I kept my smile hidden during the car ride to wherever we were going, thinking back on Aunt Lulu's reaction.

"Where's Jules?" I asked.

"She's at home and knows everything. As much as I wanted her here with us, because this concerns her, she made a strong argument about homework, making straight As and college applications."

I reminded myself to say thanks to Jules later for the heads up. It wouldn't have been hard to whip out my math book and been knee deep studying for a test.

Aunt Lulu brought me to a fancy breakfast place in the next town over. We spent the first twenty minutes in polite chit chat over topics like the weather and the...weather, while reading over the menu. After our meal arrived and we'd sipped our coffee and tea, she cleared her throat.

I tensed up and could barely choke down my scrambled eggs, waiting for whatever it was Aunt Lulu went through all this trouble for.

"I know several things to be true. One, I am not an easy person." She looked me right in the eye and dared me to say any differently, but the silence begged to be filled.

"Well, I wouldn't say you're not an easy person. I'd say that you're a strong personality who knows what she wants, and sometimes if people don't agree with you, then you, um, have a hard time." Aunt Lulu frowned. "I mean, usually, you find just the right words to bring them over to your side."

"Thank you." Doubt flashed across her face as if she wanted to add, "I think."

"And when you don't win them over—"

"Enough. You're rambling again."

I shrugged. "Sorry."

"Accepted. That said, I've noticed how hard you and Jules have worked over the past few years at school and filling your calendar with extra-curricular activities, which, of course, looked fantastic on all your college applications. I wanted to reward both of you in some measure."

This is where I should not ask questions, it would be considered impolite, so I finished off my scrambled eggs, laid my napkin in my lap, and quietly sipped the rest of the tea, which I didn't like. A reward from Aunt Lulu could be anything from a manicure to a cruise in the Bahamas. I was hoping for the cruise.

She puffed out her chest and practically announced to the tables around us, "When you have your date to the senior prom, I'll take you and Jules shopping for your dresses."

I should've said thank you and kept my big mouth closed. "And what if I don't have a date?"

Aunt Lulu widened her eyes and blinked rapidly. "Surely that horrifying suggestion won't be a problem. You wouldn't want to miss your prom."

As if it were a fact that anyone who didn't have a date, couldn't go to prom.

***

OVER THE NEXT FEW days, Aunt Lulu's words stayed with me, hovering over everything I did, reminding me, telling me that if I didn't have a date for prom then I wasn't worthy of going.

The next Saturday morning, I woke up before Hemingway licked my hand and whined to be let out. Carter had given up on bonding with the dog, especially after he received a slew of dates and gained sponsorship for the blog he'd started and was making money.

"What do you think, Hem?" I whispered as we went downstairs. "Is that a good idea?" My plan was to hit the mall early in hopes of finding a prom dress on sale. Maybe a style from last year? I had to have some kind of back up plan in case I didn't have a date.

Mom and Dad had beat me downstairs. We nodded and said good morning, and I brought Hemingway outside. It was really neat to watch the weeks go by and see the mornings get lighter and lighter and warmer and warmer. But with each dawn, the sense of doom grew inside me, as the senior prom drew closer and closer.

Back inside, I noticed Mom and Dad were still there.

"You want to talk?" I asked.

They nodded. Mom pursed her lips and tugged at her hair until Dad told her to quit it and that he'd just ask me. "Ever since Aunt Lulu stopped by last week and took you for breakfast, you haven't been the same."

I sank in my chair. And I thought I'd hidden it so well.

Mom's voice was shaky when she finally found her words. "I grew up with that woman, and I know how easily her words that are meant for good can bring hurt. I want you to know we're here if you want to talk."

In that moment, I saw Mom in a new light. I saw her as the younger sister, growing up in Aunt Lulu's shadow. If Lulu had always been strong and influential, then I can't imagine what she was like as an older sister and how many hurtful words she'd probably spoken to my mom over the years without even knowing. If I thought Mom never cared about me, I was wrong. She just didn't want to be like Aunt Lulu.

I waved my hand. "Everything's good, but I was wondering—what with the end of the year coming and all sorts of things that might cost money on the calendar—well, I know how hard you both work and that you probably want to go on a vacation like to the Bahamas or Jamaica or something where you can totally forget about life for a while or even forget about Aunt Lulu or forget about me and all the trouble—"

Mom gasped and Dad pounded his fist against the counter. "Now you wait one second, young lady."

I bit my lip, terrified that I'd said something wrong. "Sorry. I didn't mean it. You know me. I was just rambling. Forget about it." I walked toward the stairs. "Carry on!"

"Come back here," Dad commanded, then his voice softened. "What do you mean we want to forget all about you and any trouble you've caused?"

"I don't know. I guess I didn't really mean anything by it...I just...will we have enough money for a prom dress?" The words came out in one big rush and then I went to drumming the table and playing with my hair—anything not to look at my dad.

"Isn't it a little early for prom?" he asked, a bit clueless, like most dads.

I laughed, loud and shrilly, like Aunt Lulu on helium. "You're right. Silly question. Forget I asked."

"Regardless, I'm sure we'll have something for you."

Right. *We'll have something for you.* I knew exactly what that meant—Great Aunt Matilda's old wedding gown with the lace stripped off it or a trip to the thrift store or how about Jules's prom dress from last year?

***

I ARRIVED RIGHT WHEN the mall opened and figured I had at least one full hour of privacy. It didn't matter that I was dressed in sweats with the word dance on the butt or that my hair was up in a messy bun or that I wore absolutely no makeup. In fact, I was almost in disguise. Maybe no one would recognize me, which was perfect because I was on a reconnaissance mission, scouting out the dress possibilities, because I really didn't want to wear Great Aunt Matilda's wedding gown.

Were there dresses in my size and on sale? Could I find one on the racks from last year? I could do that. Definitely. So, my plan was perfect, except maybe I should've worn sunglasses and Mom's large floppy beach hat because toward the end of my time, right when I was about to leave, Zeke and Ava walked into the store.

There are many things to do in this situation. One, stay calm and walk out casually without anyone noticing. Two, grab a bunch of stylish clothes and act obnoxious trying them all on and then buy nothing under pretense that they don't fit right. Or three, duck behind the rack and hope for the best.

Yup. I chose three. I ducked behind the clearance rack, wondering about the light blue tulle skirt chaffing my cheek and if this dress would fit me and was it strapless or not because I wanted straps. My mistake? Not knowing that the new line of bathing suits was right behind me.

Their voices came closer, Ava's sugary flirty voice and Zeke's calm and sexy one. Not that I cared at all that they were together. Zeke is free to date or be friends with anyone he wants to. He hadn't gone out of his way to talk to me since I "chose" Jasper on Valentine's Day.

I tried not to think about that day and the look of absolute betrayal and disappointment in Zeke's eyes when I didn't have the guts to stand up to Jasper. Zeke didn't know all the extenuating circumstances like essay papers and deals and trying to make soul mates jealous even if that plan was failing miserably, and I had moved on.

"Cassidy?" Ava trilled, sounding a bit too much like Aunt Lulu. "Is that you? What are you doing on the floor?"

I wanted to say something smart and witty like, "Just bowing down before your grace," but instead, I said, "A price tag dropped."

Ava carefully fingered the dresses on the rack and understanding spread across her features. That might not happen very often for her, but it's a dangerous thing when it happens.

"Are you looking for a prom dress? Here?" She stifled a giggle. Zeke frowned, but looked on as if he wanted to know the answer too.

I shot to my feet, knocking off a few dresses. "Well, it's all the new trend. Where have you been?"

"What new trend?" Her words were sharp and demanding because if there was a new trend then she'd know about it.

"Oh, you know. The one where you buy a used or on sale prom dress and then give what you didn't spend to those youths in more unfortunate areas." I kept rambling on about charities and goodwill and to this day have no clue what I said. Don't really want to know either.

Ava cut through all my chatter. "Do you even have a date?"

It only took about three seconds to answer, but in those seconds, the past few months flashed through my head. I thought about Aunt Lulu inferring that I couldn't go to prom if I didn't have a date, and I thought about all the pressure senior prom brings to girls and I thought about the big ugly wrist corsages and that if I went by myself I wouldn't have to deal with that. I opened my mouth to say that I was going by myself and proud of it. But she spoke first.

"Oh, sorry,"—she clapped her hands to her cheeks—"what was I thinking? I didn't mean to put you on the spot. Of course, you don't have a date yet."

I bit my lip and peeked at the slight scowl on Zeke's face toward Ava. He was too nice of a guy to be with her. At the same time, I didn't want his pity, and I couldn't let her have the last word.

"Actually, I'm going with Jasper." Even I had to hide the noise coming out of my mouth as we both gasped at the same time.

Zeke's slight scowl turned to surprise then disappointment. I wanted to break down and tell him the whole truth over hot chocolate and a raspberry Danish at the food court. I hadn't wanted to turn him down on Valentine's Day.

"You're going with Jasper?" Her face paled, and I thought she might faint.

"Yup. Now if you don't mind, I need to make a purchase and get going." This was where I really needed to stop talking. "Jasper's expecting me soon."

I grabbed the light blue tulle dress, which turned out later to be four sizes too small and non-returnable, then I marched up and spent the last of my Christmas money on a dress I probably wouldn't wear.

On my way out of the store, I caught Zeke looking at me while Ava bored him to death with fashion details, while holding up this cute light blue two-piece. This time I couldn't read his expression so scurried out of the store, wishing I had something cooler written on my butt, like *cool* or *cute* or *yes I ramble and I just lied so please forgive me*.

Not that he cared, so it totally didn't matter.

CHAPTER 26

I PULLED INTO JASPER'S driveway and shut off Mom's minivan. I parked next to a Hummer in front of his mansion with all sorts of windows and dormers and additions. Hesitantly, I made my way to the front door.

A beautiful woman with smiley eyes opened the door. "May I help you?"

I tried peeking in behind her, but the insides were in shadows compared to the bright midday sun. "Is Jasper here?"

"Why, yes. Come on in." She ushered me inside. "We're just sitting down to a pancake brunch. Please join us."

I walked into the kitchen to find the entire family sitting down. Jasper had four younger brothers and sisters, and everything looked rather normal. I almost expected a plethora of servants dressed in tuxes and tap dancing while serving hot chocolate. But other than the gleaming stainless steel of new appliances, it didn't feel any different than my family brunches.

Jasper's cold, steely eyes found mine, urging me to leave now.

"Um, maybe I should leave. I didn't mean to interrupt."

"That's right," Jasper said. "You should leave."

Before he said that with condemnation in his tone, I might've found a way to exit gracefully. Any number of excuses would've done the trick. Hemingway came to mind. He was probably waiting for me to take him for a walk.

His dad picked up on it right away. "Jasper, that's no way to welcome a friend. And who is this lovely young lady?"

After sending a warning to Jasper with just my eyes, I strode across the floor with as much confidence I could muster. After all, I was still wearing Carter's T-shirt and sweats with words on the butt that now I was wishing said *don't make me mad because you'll regret it*. I stuck out my hand and firmly shook Jasper's dad's hand.

"I'm Cassidy, Jasper's girlfriend."

Jasper coughed and almost choked on the orange juice he was drinking.

"What?" his mom exclaimed as if Jasper never brought any girls home. "What a treat." She pulled out the chair across from Jasper. "You must join us for pancakes. They're Jasper's favorite."

"Why thank you so much. Jasper has been hinting forever that he'd like to invite me over but to tell you the truth, I think he was a little nervous."

His brothers and sisters giggled. Jasper kicked me under the table.

His mother sat next to his father. "I'm Maryanne and this is Jasper Senior. And you are welcome anytime. Why don't you tell us a little bit about yourself?"

Jasper smiled—quite evilly, I might add. "Yes, Cassidy. Why don't you tell us about yourself."

"Well, um, I…"

Jasper leaned back with his arms folded across his chest to enjoy the show.

"I live at home with my parents and my twin brother. We're just a normal family. I've been studying hard in hopes of receiving a college scholarship to help my parents out…"

My enthusiasm to lie dwindled. Of course, I cared about all those things but his mom smiled at me with such trust and interest I couldn't keep going. It didn't mean I was going to leave and make life easier for Jasper. It just meant I needed to change my approach and turn up the heat on my so-called boyfriend.

"Why don't I tell you how Jasper and I met?"

"We'd love that," his mom said.

"I'm not sure we would've ever crossed paths, since we run in somewhat different social circles."

"You can say that again," Jasper mumbled.

"But honestly, I think Jasper was tired of all the clingy social-climbing girls, so when he asked for help with his English essays, I couldn't say no. We were great friends at first and then it blossomed from there. I guess you could say my love for literature inspired him."

His mom rested her chin on her hand and sighed dreamily. "Good thing you stopped by, then."

Jasper's dad clapped him on the shoulder. "Good to hear you took my advice seriously and asked for help. You should have told us sooner."

Jasper sat up and leaned forward as if on the counter attack. I braced myself for the worst because I'd given him lots of ammunition.

"Why don't you share with my parents what happened last spring? It's quite the story." It was my turn to kick him under the table. "Oh," he said sweetly. "And she loves playing footsies with me."

I closed my eyes and breathed, trying to stop what felt like fire spreading across my face as his younger sisters laughed.

"But about last spring?" he said.

After another deep breath, I said. "That's old news. It started as me trying to help someone and slowly snowballed. I don't even know what the real story is anymore."

"No, really," Jasper said. "Tell us. I'm not sure I ever heard the entire story even after all the time we've spent together. I guess we focus too much on sentence structure. I'd love to hear it."

I took that opportunity to finish off the short stack of pancakes and links of sausage I'd been served. "Wow, this is really delicious." That wasted about two minutes.

"Cassidy, come now, no need to be shy. We're listening."

And they were. The entire family had finished and were leaning back in their chairs, their full attention on me, waiting to hear some incredible story involving me.

I'd love to tell the truth about what happened. Let everyone know that I wasn't the only criminal, but I pushed those desires deep down in the locked box I kept in my heart. But I had to say something to fill the silence.

I giggled. "I have an even better story to tell. It's actually the reason I stopped by this morning. I didn't want to keep Jasper waiting any longer."

His whole body tensed, a muscle pulsing in his jaw.

"Your son is so romantic. He knows I love romance and the stars on the nights when everything is quiet and the sky is alight with beauty. He knows my love for surprise and originality, which is something he's been working on in his writing, by the way."

His parents gave nods of approval and his brother scoffed. Jasper's cheeks were slightly tinted with pink, whether from rage or embarrassment I wasn't sure.

That's when I surprised him and reached across the table and grabbed his hand, which was fiddling with the fork. "He came over one night and surprised me with a late night stroll. He brought me to a field and asked me..." I waved my hand in front of my eyes to ward off the tears that were either a result of my romantic story or because he was squeezing my hand so tight.

His mother's hands were clasped. "Oh, please. Don't keep us waiting."

I blinked and turned my attention to Jasper. "Honey, I'd love to go to senior prom with you. My answer is yes!"

He let go of my hand and shot up from the table as his mother sighed, his father nodded in approval and his siblings giggled. He walked over to my side of the table. I thought he was going to yank me by my hair and throw me out the door. Instead, he gently gripped my arm.

"Yes and we have lots of details to work out so we'll be up in my room." He smiled at his parents, but it was tight-lipped and I feared for my life.

"How about some more of those pancakes?" I asked.

He patted my shoulder. "Now, you know what you told me about cutting down on what you eat so you can fit into your prom dress."

"Jasper. How awful of you." His mom's face paled. "Cassidy has a perfect figure. Where are your manners?"

"Well, Mom, since we're sharing news and all and personal stories, Cassidy is working on sharing her own truth about her binge eating. She's really trying to cut back and has asked me to help her." He leaned down and kissed my cheek. "Right, Cass?"

"Well, I wouldn't call it binge eating. More like—"

"You know what your therapist said about this. No down playing it."

"Oh," his mom said.

I shrugged. "He's right. I couldn't make it through the week without him." I stood. "Let's go do some planning."

"Jasper!" his mom called. "Please leave the bedroom door open."

As soon as we got into the room, I lit into him. "Binge eating? Seriously? I have problems, but eating isn't one of them. I have a perfectly healthy body image and eat lots of veggies."

He flopped on his bed and tossed a football in the air to catch and then tossed it again. "Chill. Don't want to trigger an episode, now."

I stayed at the door, fuming and embarrassed, even though I knew I deserved that and worse. Maybe I had anger management issues when it came to Ava and her snide remarks. That was more my problem. Regardless, it had been worth it just to see the shocked look on her face when I told her Jasper asked me to prom.

"Might as well sit down," he said dryly, "since we have to keep up the pretense of planning our prom date, which, of course, will never happen, because we'll 'break-up' a few weeks before prom."

"Just so you know. Finagling a date to prom with you has nothing to do with how cute you are or that all the girls want to—"

"You think I'm cute?" He tossed the football to the floor. "My day just got better. Want to make out?"

"Um, no." I ignored his pout, which made him more irresistible. "It also has nothing to do with your status in school and that every girl dreams of going to prom with you."

"Wow. You're good for my ego. You should come over every Saturday."

"Gosh, thanks but no thanks. I wouldn't want your head to explode."

He just laughed. "So why do you want to go with me then? Let me guess. Something to do with your lover boy."

"Something like that." With no other witty remarks springing to mind, I studied his room. Typical. Shelves of trophies and ribbons from all his athletic pursuits. "Where do you want to go to college?"

He eyed me warily. "Is this a trick question?"

I sat on the bed. "No, I just figured since we're going to prom we should cover some of the basics so we don't have that one slow dance where we're not sure what to say and it's awkward and we start sweating and my make-up smears...you know."

He laughed again. "You're funny."

"That's a first." No one has ever thought my rambling was funny.

"Even though you're growing on me a little and you make me laugh, we're going to have to stage a break up soon."

"Phew. I'm getting tired of writing your essays anyway."

He shrugged. "Okay, how about you write one last essay, that big one that's due in a couple weeks, and then at some point we'll have this dramatic cafeteria break up that will leave people talking for days. That'll be fun."

"A blast, I'm sure."

I left while the going was good, said goodbye to his parents, then rushed home. I had the prom date, so Aunt Lulu would take me shopping, even though it was only a temporary date. Honestly? That was okay with me, because I was so done with this charade. Especially since it had never helped with Michael one bit. If anything it had hurt our chances.

Or, I'd never had a chance anyway.

CHAPTER 27

I LOCKED THE DOOR to my room and thought about barricading it with my dresser but I didn't want to pull a muscle in my back and walk around hunched over for the rest of the week, and a part of me knew this was a futile resistance.

Someone knocked on the door. I tensed and Hemingway who is attuned to my every emotion and need, growled.

"Just me," Carter said with a sigh.

I rubbed Hemingway's ears. I'd been getting a lot of that by the way. Sighing and huffing like what I was saying was absolutely ridiculous. But most of my words had been the truth. It was my life that was bordering over the top.

"Come on, Cass. Let me in."

"Fine." I huffed, unlocked the door, peeked in the hallway, then yanked him inside.

Carter shrugged me off and crouched, calling to Hemingway. "Come here, boy. Come to Papa."

Papa? He couldn't be serious, but I could see he was with his earnest expression and cute smile. "Not going to happen. Dogs usually bond with one of their owners and that happens to be me, but you got your use out of him—all your dates. I think Hemingway is exceptionally aware of human emotions and knew that you were using him. So deal with it."

"Anyway, why are you hiding out? Aunt Lulu is waiting downstairs."

"I know. She promised to take me shopping for a dress, but I didn't know it would be the next weekend and I'm not sure I'm ready for it."

He marched over to me. "Let's go. It's just going to get worse the longer you stay up here."

"Cassidy!" Aunt Lulu trilled from downstairs. I groaned.

Carter walked me downstairs like he was the grim reaper and I was heading to my death. At the bottom of the stairs, he whispered, "You know you have always been her favorite. Hey, she's buying you a prom dress."

Somewhere between the bottom of the stairs and walking across the kitchen floor to where Aunt Lulu and my mom chatted, I went through a transformation. Carter's words hit a nerve and gratefulness rushed through me. My aunt, the one with all the money, was taking me shopping for a prom dress. I wouldn't have to wear Great Aunt

Matilda's old wedding gown with too much lace that had faded yellow with time and smelled like mothballs.

"Ready to shop?" I chirped.

Mom's expression went from tense—probably from talking to Aunt Lulu—to surprised and a little bit sad. I went over and gave her a hug. "Sure you don't want to come?"

"Well—"

"Of course not," Aunt Lulu boomed. "Your mom hates shopping and we're going to go to every store possible until we find the perfect dress. It's going to be a long, utterly exhausting but exhilarating day."

"I think I need a nap."

Aunt Lulu pinched my cheek. "You are so funny. Such a sense of humor. Now, let's get started."

What Aunt Lulu didn't realize was that I wasn't kidding. Just the idea of shopping all day made me need a power nap. Mom stood timidly next to me.

"Mom should come. I'm sure Jules won't mind." I glanced out the window at Aunt Lulu's car. "Where's Jules?"

Aunt Lulu waved her hand. "I'm taking Jules on her special trip later in this week. I supposed your mother could join us..."

Mom laughed and pulled me into a hug. "Don't worry about it. I have work to do here, and I'll hear all about it later."

The car drive over was filled with Aunt Lulu's shopping advice, and let me tell you, she should write a book on it.

First, she shoved a water bottle at me and told me to drink half of it by the time we arrived at the mall. "There's an art to keeping hydrated."

She proceeded to explain that it's best to drink just enough that you're not parched in the middle of Macy's but not so much that you're in a dressing room with a pile of clothes, standing in your unmentionables and suddenly have to use the little girls' room. Mainly because that would waste prime shopping time. If I drank half the bottle, then my tinkle break would come after we were done with the first store. It was all about timing.

"What if the first dress I try on is the one?" I asked, timidly, knowing that it's always a risk to say anything to Aunt Lulu when she's on a roll.

She did this gasp/flutter thing with her voice. "Nonsense! The first one is *never* the one. You have to have comparison."

She went on to tell me that we'll never know which one is the perfect dress until we try on all sorts of different colors and styles. Even the ones I hate, I should try on, because you just never know. Dresses can look different on than off.

"Even the pink zebra-striped nylon stretchy dress with feathers on the sleeves?"

Aunt Lulu smiled. "Even the pink zebra-striped nylon stretchy dress with feathers on the sleeves and sequins on the derriere."

Okay, she totally upped me on that one.

Another rule was to keep focused. We were there for a prom dress and that had to take precedence, because the next weekend the dress that was *the one* could be gone from a store we didn't get to. So no side trips to look at necklaces on sales or at the new Spanx that promised to make anyone look like a size eight. I hoped she was talking about herself there.

She might've said something about dressing room strategies and the perfect number of dresses to try on at a time but I'd zoned out and couldn't help but think about my date and that prom was going to be nothing like I'd always imagined.

In the first store, we went directly to the prom dress section and it was like heaven opened up from above. I saw it. *The one.* It was pink and had tulle and a shimmery material over it with tiny little sequins in the dress part. The top part was a simple pale pink satin with spaghetti straps. My heart did this funny little beat like I just ran into the guy of my dreams.

I lost all focus and forgot all the rules because I had to touch the dress, feel it between my fingers and hold it against my cheek. I needed a moment to fantasize and do some visual imagery.

The dress was just within reach, when Aunt Lulu pulled me in the other direction. "If that's the first dress you like, then it's not the one." She stacked ten dresses on the cart that paled in comparison and shooed me into the dressing rooms.

I went back to the dress and ran my fingers over the pale pink satin material. "I'll try on every single one of these, but I've got to try on this one, too."

"Trust me, darling. I know what I'm talking about here." Then she pulled me toward the dressing room.

I tried on every single one—just to make her happy. And even though some weren't bad, they weren't *the one* that made my heart go pitter-patter, the one that I'd dance around my room wearing, pretending.

When I said no to ones that Aunt Lulu thought were gorgeous—with a strong emphasis on the first syllable—she brought in dresses of different styles. See, another one of her rules was that after the initial shop around, I stay in the dressing room, while she, or I should say while a worker brought in more dresses.

They never brought in the one.

We went to five other stores, and I couldn't find a single dress that matched the first one I found even though that broke Aunt Lulu's rule. After we left our sixth store, and even though Aunt Lulu's hair was a bit on the frizz, and her lipstick was fading, I said, "Why don't we go back to that first store?"

Aunt Lulu gave a little huff where her cheeks ballooned out for a second before she finally breathed, probably trying to garner self control so she didn't wring my neck. "Fine, let's go."

We walked back toward the first store, where I'd seen *the one*. As we drew closer, I walked faster, my arms swinging, and believe me, I had focus. A driving need to slip into the gown, knowing it would fit me like silk on a fairy princess. Even Aunt Lulu was rather out of breath when we arrived.

For the first time that day, I took the lead. Aunt Lulu might've argued or taken over but she could barely get a word between breaths. I almost suggested she join the early morning walking group that met in the mall every morning.

I rushed past the shoes, the kiddy department, the makeup counters and didn't even look. I weaved in between the dresses until I found the rack. The pink sparkled under the lights and the satin glimmered, waiting for me. I arrived, slightly out of breath and wondering if we should've eaten more than a power bar and an apple. With a happy sigh I ran my fingers over the material and brought the smooth satin up to my cheek.

"But this was the first one," Aunt Lulu mentioned in a strained voice.

"It's not the first one anymore. It's the last one. Technically, I never tried it on. Remember?"

"Oh, right." She fanned her face, probably realizing from my half-growl-way of talking that we were adding amendments to her rules. "Okay, off you go. Size six, right?" She flipped through the dresses. She kept flipping and flipping and flipping and then flipped again. She bit her lip and beads of sweat appeared on her upper lip. "Are you sure you're not a size 4?"

I shook my head, stumbling back until I bumped into a rack of dresses, knocking half of them to the floor in a pile of soft colors and fabrics. I only stared, then stumbled back some more until I fell into a chair. I leaned over, breathing, trying to stop a self-induced panic attack.

The size six dress was gone. While I pandered to Aunt Lulu's rules, someone came in and stole my dress. *The one.*

Minutes later, Aunt Lulu said, "Here we go." She held the dress in her hand but one look at her face and the nervous twitching of her lips told me it was the wrong size. And I was right. In the dressing room, I zipped it up only to have my ribcage crushed.

"Not working," I said in a breathy voice, my heart crushed to bits. "Can we just go home? I think I'm done for the day."

"Yes, dear." Then I think she added this rule just for me. "Sometimes when we're tired and have put in a full day, we need to know when to admit defeat and go out for ice cream."

Okay, sometimes my Aunt Lulu can be almost cool. That was when it hit me that she'd given up her whole day for me. That even though it was a drop in the bucket for her, she was spending her money on me. She'd given up lots of her time all year for me.

For the first time that day, there was silence on the other side of the door and silence in the dressing room. I sucked it up. "Aunt Lulu, was there a dress in this store you thought looked good on me?"

"I'll be right back." Her heels clicked away. Maybe she should add wear sensible shoes when shopping all day to her rules.

I tried to get *the one* that was in the wrong size off. I reached in the back and tugged on the zipper, but it stuck. I sank to my knees in the one that was not the one and waited.

A few minutes later, a puff of yellow satin and crinoline came flying over the door. I saw it through a blur and barely remembered trying it on earlier. I tugged and tugged at the zipper, fighting the tears, almost ready to ask for help. At the last second, it came loose and I forced it off.

Quietly, I dressed, without trying the yellow one on. I didn't have the heart. I couldn't see past the pale pink satin gown that I wouldn't wear. My feet hurt. My stomach growled. And I felt like a zombie shuffling through the streets.

Part way home I had to admit. "Aunt Lulu, thanks for the offer of ice cream, but I think I'd just like to go home. Maybe another day."

"Sure thing, honey."

She didn't say one word on the drive to my house. Maybe she felt like a shopping zombie too. We trudged into the house and Aunt Lulu forced her enthusiasm, even though I knew she was drained too. "We're back and found *the one!*"

She unzipped it for my mom and dad and Carter to see. The puffs of yellow spilled out, especially the ginormous poofy flower on the right shoulder. I was finally able to really look at the dress I ended up with, that I could only be grateful for...and it was awful. The bright yellow would make my skin look pale and my hair dull. The skirt was just the amount of poofy that it was too much and little girlish.

I blinked furiously, then wrapped my arms around Aunt Lulu before I lost it. I barely held it together and hoped she took my emotion as gratefulness, which made me feel even worse. "Thank you so much. I appreciate everything." I pulled back. "But I'm really tired."

She patted my cheek, her eyes misty. "Anytime, dear."

***

LATE THAT NIGHT AFTER three grilled cheese sandwiches and chocolate milk, I stole into the backyard. Somehow I'd hoped that the full moon would create enough of a romantic atmosphere that my mood would lighten and I could find the positive in all this.

The screen door squeaked. "May I join you?" Mom asked.

"Of course." I lay back in the lounge chair and closed my eyes so she couldn't see all the different thoughts and emotions swirling through me. My mom has this radar, this special way of knowing when I'm upset.

She sat on the edge of the chair and took my hand in hers. The simple act, the simple gesture caused a sob to break through, a hiccup really.

"I should've been stronger this morning and gone, but you seem to have developed this special bond with Aunt Lulu this year and I didn't want to squash that."

It wasn't about some special bond. "Aunt Lulu had taken me on as her project. Buying the prom dress was just following through."

"No, I don't think so."

I opened my eyes. "What do you mean?"

Even though the moon was bright, the light was soft and fell around my mom. She had an ethereal beauty about her. "I mean you're more than a project. She loves you and that's how she shows love. It just took me years to understand my sister was never tearing me down with her advice but trying to love me in her own way. She loves fiercely, and how better to show that than an all day shopping trip."

And buying me a dress even though it's not *the one*. Knowing that the dress was her love for me meant I could never take it back or change my mind or wear another one. I fell into my mom's arms and let her hug away my tears.

"Even though I love Aunt Lulu, I'm so glad she's not my mom."

Mom laughed and hugged me tighter. "Me too."

CHAPTER 28

THE SPRING OF MY senior year was passing by way too quickly. So many things were happening like senior pictures and yearbook committees and final prom committee meetings.

The so-called break-up Jasper and I were supposed to stage in the cafeteria never happened. My feelings toward Jasper sank to new lows every day. Sometimes he was a complete snob and other times he would decide he didn't mind having me around.

It was one of those times, when I was simmering in a place of pain, licking my wounds from his short words with me that I wrote the final essay for him. Yeah, I probably should've waited for another time, but it felt good to unleash my pain.

Totally regretted it.

It was a Friday, the day before senior prom. The year had flown by and so many of us had senioritis. Mr. Troller stood and cleared his throat. He loosened the bow tie at his neck.

"It isn't often I receive an essay from a student filled with such personal insight and transcendence that I'm moved to tears." He got choked up and had to take a few breaths. "Teachers work and live for those few moments where they see a student grow beyond themselves. I've asked this student if he would read his essay aloud to the class and he agreed."

Everyone whispered—thankfully for the first time that day or even that week it wasn't about me—and peered around. But then Jasper stood and swaggered to the front of the room, his chest puffed out and that glory smile splattered on his face. That's when I knew that he'd grown comfortable, trusting me, and had never read my essay.

I didn't remember exactly what I'd said, but I knew it wouldn't make him look good. And that would be bad for me. Hot needle pricks of panic spread all over and the temperature in the room went through the roof and into outer space. In desperation, I shot my hand up, waving frantically.

Jasper narrowed his eyes as if suspicious that I was trying to steal his limelight. I shook my head at him, silently begging him to decline or get a sudden case of laryngitis.

"Yes, Cassidy. Do you have something to add?"

"Just in case anyone else feels bad, I want everyone to realize that sometimes when writing personal narratives we write from a *place of pain* or privacy, say when our *feelings have been hurt*, but it turns out the insight *never should've been shared.*" I ran out of words because Jasper clearly wasn't getting my message and the whole class was just staring at the girl talking nonsense, and Mr. Troller was tugging violently on his bow tie. "Sorry!" I squeaked. "Carry on."

I slumped low in my seat, closed my eyes, and listened to what would be the end of my life.

Jasper paused, then started to read. "My life has been one of privilege that few ever hope to have. I've never had to work hard for anything and my parents hand me almost everything I want. Most would think this would be a bad thing, but no, instead, this golden touch on my life has blessed me with a sense of humor and compassion."

He took a breath, pausing. I cracked an eye and noticed that he looked confused as if he couldn't quite understand if what he was reading was serious or not.

"For example, when I bless girls with my smile throughout the day, I give them hope that someday I might ask them out. When I wear my rolled-up khakis with moccasins even though it went out of style twenty years ago"—his hand started trembling causing the page to shake—"I show everyone that we should never be afraid to be ourselves and that means dressing however we'd like. But we should never carry…this…too far by lying and …"

Then he started mumbling.

"Jasper, please speak clearly. We missed a section. Why don't you back up?"

But he didn't back up. He kept on reading and he kept on reading faster as his face got redder and the whispers got louder. He zipped through until at the very end he was practically spitting out each word.

"That's why even though I said privilege was a blessing, it's really a curse because it blinds me to the true nature of life and those around me. I will continue to work hard everyday to overcome this."

Slowly, he lowered the paper, his eyes zeroing in on me. He trembled, his body a tight fist of rage, barely controlled, barely masked.

"Thank you, Jasper. And that class is an example of bravery..." The teacher blabbed on about the essay while Jasper stood, his gaze still piercing right through me.

Okay, I figured he'd be mad but I never meant him to read this aloud to the whole class and until now it had stayed sorta hazy in my mind because I was so hurt and tired. That's what I meant about writing from a place of pain.

As soon as the bell rang, I zipped out of there so fast, I could've been a super hero. I didn't go back to my locker and I took the long routes to all my classes. At one point, I hid in the guidance office and then walked to class late. After receiving my second detention, I made a decision. Time for me to be proactive.

Jasper wanted drama? He'd get girl drama to the extreme. And there's no way he could strangle me to death with slimy spaghetti and meatballs or stab me with a fork with hundreds of witnesses around.

I slammed open the lunch room doors, the sound barely making a dent in the lunchroom chatter. Gosh, this would be harder than I thought. Screwing my face up into one of extreme hurt, I stormed over to our lunch table and with one swipe, knocked his tray to the floor. We were, in fact, having spaghetti and meatballs and the sauce splattered Ava's shirt.

The clatter of the tray and Ava's shriek started to capture everyone's attention. Everyone at the table stared with various expressions of shock.

I opened my mouth, ready to spurt all sorts of lies about Jasper and how he was too controlling and I couldn't take it anymore. How I needed space and I didn't have to tell him where I was every second of the day or how many calories were in my dinner the night before.

But in that one moment, I remembered all the times he was nice. I remembered being at his house and his family and how he laughed at my ramblings. I remembered that I was the one who approached him in the bathroom and suggested our arrangement. And I remembered he said I was cute.

"Cassidy? Are you okay?" Jules asked.

I couldn't do it. I couldn't be that mean. So in a normal voice instead of going all drama queen on him, I said. "Jasper, this isn't working for me anymore. I'm just not ready to say I love you back, and that's when I realized we should probably take a break."

Okay, so I got in a little jab. Big deal. He seemed to like my sense of humor.

I didn't even look at his face. I whirled around and left the lunchroom, walking faster and faster as I approached the exit, expecting at any second for him to grab my arm and force the truth from me.

But I made it outside safely. I went straight to the nurse's office and called home, saying I felt the beginnings of a scratchy throat, and with prom the next day, I didn't want to start an epidemic.

At home, I ignored all texts and voice messages and drank tea and honey. I slept on the couch, wrapped up in a blanket, trying to avoid the fact that I hadn't thought through my actions.

Without Jasper, I didn't have a date to prom.

Late in the afternoon, Jules stopped by. I was outside, soaking the last warmth of the day. "Hey, don't worry. I'm okay. I'll make prom tomorrow."

"Oh, I know you're okay." She dropped a basket full of first aid supplies on the patio next to me. "But I decided to drop this by just in case."

Her eyes flashed, and I knew she was beyond furious.

"I know you're thinking I shouldn't have called Jasper out like that, but it really could've been much worse,

I promise." I didn't stop to take a breath. "My original plans were to make it seem like a really bad break-up and everyone would ooh and aah but I couldn't do it..."

Jules eyes were like a cold winter day, ice balls, sharp and cold. "Does everything always have to be about you?"

Huh? "Trust me, nothing is about me."

She held up her finger, refusing to listen. "We've always been close but I'm finding it hard to summon up feelings of closeness right now. You embarrassed me. You embarrassed our friends. And you embarrassed Jasper, and why?" She paced the patio, barely able to look at me. "I have no idea, so please, explain."

Where did I start? I could tell her about my deal with Jasper, or about how Michael had rejected me all year, or how Zeke caused all these weird twisty feeling inside me even though he wasn't really talking to me or how I had a yellow poofy dress with humongous flower on the shoulder that I had to wear because of all the time her mom had spent with me, and how it didn't matter because I wasn't even going to prom.

I could tell her all that. But words failed me. Somehow I knew that all those reasons would be like dandelion fluff in the wind, meaningless. That somewhere underneath that tsunami of crap was the truth, but I didn't know how to dig it out.

"You know what? I don't want to know." She lowered her voice. "I love you. You're my best friend. I'm sorry this year has been kind of strange, and I know I'm partly to blame. But as far as prom night is concerned, I'm not sure you should travel with us, especially since Jasper will be there. So when my mom insists you ride in the limo with us tomorrow, maybe..."

I got the message loud and clear. "Don't worry. I'll have other plans."

***

LATER THAT NIGHT, WELL past dark, I still sat on the porch. Mom brought out a blanket and more tea with honey, but I promised it was just nerves over prom. She understands me and even when she doesn't, she knows when to give me room. She's just awesome like that.

I was about to go in when I heard a shuffle in the trees, almost like an animal. Do we have bears? Or mountain lions? I shook it off only moments later to hear steps on the patio, and I wasn't imagining it.

"Cassidy?"

My heart stopped beating and almost fell through the floor. It was Michael. He was visiting me, pointy ears and everything.

"I understand if you don't want to talk to me." He stepped backwards. "I'll see you later."

"Um, no. I mean, you can stay. Sure."

He shuffled forward and sat next to me. We looked up into the sky at the stars, twinkling, and the clouds skimming across them. I wasn't up to idle chatter. "Is there a reason you stopped by?"

He clasped his hands and twisted them. "I know it's late and it's almost the end of the year, but I wanted to say I was sorry for blowing off our friendship."

Wow. I didn't know what to say. My heart started this little pitter patter, sparking old dreams, ones I'd sworn off.

"I understand if you don't want to be friends."

Friends? Well, friends would be a good place to start. "No, that's okay. Everyone makes mistakes and uses bad judgment at times. I don't judge any one."

He smiled, the moonlight reflecting off his glasses. I still thought he was one of the most underrated guys in the school. Someday, he was going to be a knockout running his own computer company. I knew it.

He cleared his throat a couple times. "I'm thinking that after what happened at lunch, you know, with you and Jasper, that you might be out of a prom date."

Oh. My. God. My throat almost closed up and I had to sit up and put my head between my legs, breathing in and out. I couldn't believe this was happening to me. Me! Cassidy! The girl who never gets what she wants even when she least expects it. Or doesn't want it anymore.

I steadied myself and sat back up. "Yup. I mean, yes, you're correct."

He waited, stretching the moment out while I wanted the band to strike the chorus and balloons and confetti to fall from the sky.

"Would you like to go to prom with me?"

My breath hitched and my throat ached as I fought back the sudden emotion. I tried to ignore the tiny bit of sadness that I'd pushed Zeke away all year. A few months ago I would've been doing the happy dance—on the inside. But now, I was just happy to have my friend back. "Yes, I'd love to go with you."

"Great!" He smiled, all his attention on me.

We chatted a bit more and said goodnight. At the edge of the woods he stopped. "A group of kids are going in together for a limo..."

Limo? "Yeah, I think Jules's and her friends are."

"I was thinking we could join that group. What do you think? Could you talk to Jules?"

I swallowed hard, trying to wet my throat, which had gone dry at the mention of the limo. "Well...after what happened at lunch today, I'm not so sure Jules would want me there." In fact, I knew she didn't. His body sagged and he looked absolutely crestfallen. Even though I'd moved on from Michael, I couldn't stand that look. "Ya know what? Let's go anyway." I laughed and waved the whole thing off. "I'm sure she won't mind us showing up."

"Really?" His whole face brightened up.

"Really." Oh gosh, what had I just done? No way would she let us ride in the limo.

"Great. I'll pick you up tomorrow." Then he left, practically skipping into the woods.

When I used to daydream about Michael asking me out and then asking me to prom, I was naïve. I saw that now. I invented some pretend bond between us based on how long I'd known him, and because I talked with him at his window a few times—uninvited.

When I was at camp last summer, setting my goals for the year, I stupidly included my great romance with Michael in it. But never once did I think he'd use my connections to Jules in order to be with Elena.

Connections, unfortunately, that had been severed that afternoon.

CHAPTER 29

I NEEDED A FEW moments. Okay, more like a thousand. Many different thoughts and ideas swirled through my brain, and I wasn't liking all of them. That was why I needed time to sit and be myself, not thinking of who was around or who I needed to impress or who was watching to see if I was cool enough to be their friend.

I sat on the middle of my bed, the canopy flowing around me. An array of chocolates from a Valentine box I found in a kitchen cupboard—sorry, Mom—in front of me, thinking on this past year. Hemingway lay at the foot of the bed, eyeing the chocolates and licking his chops.

"You know dogs can't eat chocolate. Sorry, Hem," I whispered, then went back to my meditative pose, after popping another chocolate, this time with cherry filling.

Today was prom. I was about to experience the pinnacle, the peak, the biggest moment of my high school life. Tonight, along with my classmates, some of whom I'd known since kindergarten, I'd waltz into the glorified gymnasium and experience the beginning of the end. With graduation only a couple weeks away, we were close to saying goodbye.

I breathed in and I breathed out. I was trying to ignore this feeling in my gut that kept trying to tell me something. I just didn't know what, and I wasn't sure I wanted to know.

"Hey!" Carter poked his head into my room. "Shouldn't you be getting ready? Like at least take a shower?"

He was already dressed in a tux, except it wasn't a normal tux. I popped another chocolate, this time caramel, and motioned him into my room. "Is that what I think it is?"

A big grin spread across his face, lighting up his eyes. "Yup."

I gave up on meditation, because I had to touch him. That sounds really bad but this was his final masterpiece, anyone would want to touch him. "When did you do this?"

He stroked the sleeve made completely from duct tape. "A bit at a time all year. Unfortunately, I couldn't quite figure out the zipper part so I couldn't use the pants."

"That. Is. Awesome." I was sure this latest stunt would get him like a zillion more dates. "Your weekends will be booked until the end of summer."

He shrugged. "You're really going with Michael?"

I flopped backward against my pillow. "I guess so."

He swiped the chocolate wrappers to the floor and sat on my bed. "Sorry. I hate to break it to you, but true love isn't everything it's cracked up to be." He gave me a hug and moved to the door.

I didn't have to explain anything to him. He knew Michael and I going to prom had nothing to do with love or romantic sighs or kisses in the moonlight. Absolutely nothing.

He smiled. "Try to have a good time."

When he left I knew I couldn't stall any longer. At some point, I'd have to open the dress bag and look at my dress—even put it on. I was hoping it wasn't as bad as I remembered, because I hadn't looked at it since my shopping trip with Aunt Lulu.

I showered, primped, used tons of vanilla-scented lotion, and stood in front of my closet in my strapless bra and granny underwear. Tonight was about being comfortable and no one would see underwear lines in the poofy monstrosity I'd be wearing.

"Cassidy! Leave time for pictures!" Mom called up the stairs.

"Okay!" I yelled back.

Pictures are moments in time that in the future when we look back will encapsulate a memory of an entire night. It's what we'll show to our future husbands and our children or our pet goldfish. They'll ask about the night and we'll show them pictures. They won't know or be able to see the heartache behind yellow dresses and limos and prom dates.

It was time. With a deep breath, I slowly unzipped the bag. Puffy swathes of yellow silk spilled out. The flower on the shoulder was even bigger than I remembered. It was a disaster. I hadn't imagined it.

"Michael's here!" Mom called.

I got dressed, not bothering to glance in the mirror because I didn't want to give into my craving for double fudge nut ice cream just to feel better. Yes. I totally admit to eating ice cream during times of emotional duress.

I wanted to feel like a princess in her ball gown, sweeping down the stairs in a cloud of glitter and sunshine. Instead, I felt like a baby duckling or an overgrown flowerbed in need of weeding.

Michael waited at the bottom. Mom and Dad stood next to him, oohing and aahing. She snapped a billion pictures, and I understood why Carter left early. She made us pose inside and outside, in front of the flowerbed, in front of the porch, and peeking out from behind a tree.

She gave me a huge hug before we left and whispered in my ear. "Remember. It's not what you look like. It's not the clothes or dress you wear. It's not how well you do your make-up that makes you beautiful."

Right, Mom. What planet do you live on? I fake-smiled and whispered thanks.

Michael was a perfect gentleman, holding my arm and opening the door to his mom's Honda. Then we were driving toward Jules's and I wanted to puke. I counted the telephone poles we passed, and as we got closer a sense of doom fell on me.

"Are you sure you want to ride in a limo? I think limos are way overrated and sensationalized. It's really a marketing gimmick, so teens think their prom experience isn't complete without it. And do we really want to be a part of that kind of brainwashing marketing scam?"

I stopped talking. Michael's face looked rather pale, and he gripped the steering wheel like he was in the Indy 500.

I laughed. "Never mind. Just joking. I've been watching way too many documentaries on the big marketing schemes in corporate America."

More silence.

"So, nice weather, huh? For a while there, I was afraid it was going to rain, not that guys have to worry about that, but you know, hair and makeup. The whole prom experience could be ruined by inclement weather." I laughed again, which was beginning to annoy even me. "Yeah, so good weather."

Then I took to looking out the window and thinking about anything and everything except what was about to happen.

"This isn't a good idea, is it?" Michael finally said.

He took his eyes off the road for a second, but that second was enough for me to dip into his soul and taste and feel the hope and longing there. Hope and longing I had felt for months when it came to this boy. A part of me, no matter how hurt I was that he blew me off this past year and went after one of my friends, didn't want him to experience that bitter crushing disappointment when hope is snuffed out and replaced by lies and yellow dresses.

"I'm not sure. I guess we'll find out."

I didn't, couldn't say anything else as we pulled into Jules's driveway. The white stretch limo gleamed in the late afternoon sun, spit and polished until it shined.

I found my happy place, the place where I don't care what everyone else thinks. "Let's go."

Of course, Aunt Lulu rushed over to me, gushing about the dress and my hair and makeup. "I didn't expect you! What a surprise." She welcomed Michael. "All the kids are on the back porch with some appetizers. The professional photographer should be here any second."

When we walked onto the back porch, silence fell, except for the rather loud crinkle of my dress. I knew they were staring at the god-awful poofy flowers on my shoulder and were secretly cringing or laughing on the inside. Or questioning whether I was truly related to Jules.

But then I saw something pink and glittery and satin with spaghetti straps and my breath whooshed out of me. I stumbled back, spots dancing in my periphery.

Michael jumped in to help me. "Are you okay?"

"I'm fine." I took a couple sobbing breaths that I hoped no one noticed and thought maybe it had been my imagination. But when I looked again, it was still there. My dress. My beautiful pink satin dress with the shimmery skirt and fairy tale glitter.

And she was talking about it to Zeke who looked bored out of his mind. "And I was so lucky because this dress was the last in my size and they weren't restocking. It was like it was meant for me."

I kinda zoned out after that, numb to the sparkle and glitter of prom.

Jules didn't say one word. She nodded in welcome then went back to conversing with Jasper. Michael pulled out a seat for me and made small talk for a little bit, but eventually, bit by bit, gravitated toward Elena.

I nibbled on fancy cheese and rye crackers and looked anywhere but at the dress. Yeah, sure I could write a novel about each person there and my complicated history with them. I could've spent days observing Zeke and Ava flirt and talk, wondering how he ended up with someone like her. I could've camped out with a bag of chips and watched Jules and Jasper and figured out how they ended up going together. But I watched Michael. And I watched Elena.

Her eyes seemed brighter and a little bit twinkly, like the stars Michael loves. She had this giggly floaty aura about her every time he leaned forward to whisper some intimate joke that was just between them. It was like, when Michael strode through with that hot-but-dorky look he gets away with, she remembered all the incredibly nice things he'd done for her that year. Things I wished he'd done for me.

Maybe she was caught up in the whole prom thing, but I think she finally liked him and just couldn't fully go for it because he was a cute geek, and she'd finally made it into the "it" crowd.

I brushed the cracker crumbs from my dress and didn't even try to break into the conversations. They laughed and joked and talked around me, but it was like I was in my own little bubble, floating there, and no one saw me.

Zeke flashed his concern a couple times toward me, but Ava pulled him right back in. Ava and her pink glitter satin dress. Jasper and Jules didn't look once after they'd said hello, but in the brief half-second I devoted to him, I noticed the tense way he sat with his shoulders all knotted up and his strained smile. He kept fiddling with the silverware, and I worried briefly whether he was going to throw a knife at my chest.

Finally, the photographer arrived and we went through a series of poses again. I tried to stay out of as many as possible, more out of respect for Jules. I was here for Michael, not for myself.

With a shrill call, Aunt Lulu ushered us out to the limo. She and Uncle Rudie were heading out for a night on the town in her car. She gave me an extra squeeze. "You look absolutely beautiful in that dress."

After some more pictures, everyone climbed inside. It was Michael and Elena and me left standing outside. The group in the limo had already popped the fake bubbly and were passing it around.

I caught Elena's arm before she climbed inside and motioned for Michael to come here. "Listen, guys. I'm going to do you both a favor." I looked at Elena. "You'd have to be stupid not to realize that this guy is totally crazy for you." I fought off the rush of emotion. "Don't you realize he's a hot geek? I can tell you like him, and I think you should give him a chance. I don't know why your date didn't show or why you said no to Michael—"

"He never asked," Elena said, a tinge of hurt behind her words.

I stared at Michael. "Seriously? You've been after her all year and you never asked her to *prom*?"

He scuffed his shoe against a stone in the driveway. "I didn't think she'd say yes."

Elena reached for his hand. "I waited, hoping you'd ask. I said no to others, hoping. Finally, Jules said I could ride with them."

"That settles it then." I took a deep breath and said the hardest words I'd ever spoken in my life. I had to start several times before I got the sentence out. "You two were meant to go together."

Elena hugged me. "Really? You mean it?"

I nodded. "I don't think there's room for me and my dress in there anyway." I laughed when I wanted to sob.

Elena climbed into the limo, squealing with her news. I swallowed the lump in my throat.

"I'm sure there's room for you too," Michael said with a shy smile.

I knew all along Michael was a nice guy, and this just proved it. But the idea of squishing into the corner, the odd girl out, with my yellow flower hitting the person next to me in the face every time I moved, plus the fact that Jules didn't want me, made me take a step back. "No thanks."

He handed me his keys. "Then take my car."

"Sure."

The limo pulled out and I stood in the driveway, more thoughts and ideas swirling, but I still wasn't able to quite figure them out. But one thought kept cropping up, and I couldn't say no to it. Maybe it was desperation. Maybe it was that at that moment I felt completely powerless. I ducked inside their house and grabbed the key from the kitchen.

Minutes later, I sat in Uncle Rudie's Porsche. All the power was at my fingertips. My fingers shook as I gripped the wheel and the garage door opened, the late afternoon sunshine spilling through.

CHAPTER 30

Uncle Rudie's Porsche was like a dream. Every time I barely pressed on the gas it zoomed forward, like a spaceship through the Milky Way. On the drive to the school, I figured out why my uncle loves this car and keeps it hidden away most of the year. This car is an escape. Like a fantasy novel, or triple-decker ice cream, or pink satin dresses. Except way more expensive. This car sucks away your problems and injects you with the power to make decisions.

I pulled into the high school parking lot and made the first one. I parked way in the back corner of the lot because the idea of some careless driver dinging the side made me feel sick. Once I locked the door and patted the sides, then wiped off the fingerprints it left, I made another decision. This was my senior prom. Even if it turned out nothing like I expected, I was going to own it, big poofy yellow dress with the obnoxious flower on my shoulder and all.

We'd spent months planning, purchasing supplies, and then decorating the gym according to my brilliant idea of a fairy tale prom, which was really Jules's. Uncle Rudie had paid for a construction company to build and paint what looked like the outside of a castle at the entrance. The insides of the gym brought me back hundreds of years. Fake torches flickered and chandeliers hung from the ceiling. Plastic sheets on the walls made the interior like the stone walls of a castle. And in the middle was Carter's armor on a mannequin, plastic sword and shield and all. Just for a moment, I could take a breath in and pretend this was a fairy tale.

The only problem with being confident in the decision to go solo and own it is that everyone else is caught up with their date, giggling, flirting, and tugging their strapless dresses up, which is why I wanted the whole spaghetti strap approach.

But who came up with the rule that girls had to have dates to go to prom to have a rewarding experience?

I wanted to know, because the date deal turned out to be a big scam. There's the whole gigantic wrist corsage thing, and the stress of wondering if your pits smell halfway through a dance.

But going alone wasn't so hot either. There was the stab of jealousy and heart wrenching experience of watching a certain guy dance with another girl. I'm not going to mention any names, because it had been my choice.

I hid among the shadows, only making an appearance here and there. I danced a few times with boys from my classes and tried not to knock them out with my huge flower. I danced alongside Elena, but Zeke and Ava always seemed to be close by. I nibbled at the appetizers, but all I could manage was sips of Sprite because the realization that I'd taken Uncle Rudie's Porsche was not sitting well in my stomach. At all.

By the middle of prom I was plain ole depressed. My feet hurt in the tiny heels Aunt Lulu made me wear, and it was an emotional marathon watching everyone.

I slipped over the drawbridge and into the warm spring air. I couldn't help but think of last spring at this time. I sat on the steps and stared up at the starry canvas, painted with my dreams, each and every little one scattered among bears, lions, and dippers. I didn't move for quite awhile, caught up in the awe and beauty.

I barely heard the movement behind me until Jasper spoke in that low, commanding voice of his that might work on the football field but just ticked me off. "Nice night."

I sighed, crashing back to reality. "What do you want Jasper?"

"A dance, of course."

He narrowed his eyes, all the flirt and fun gone. I crossed my arms and tapped my foot. We had the ultimate stare down, me, the lowly peon, versus the high and mighty

Lord of the manor. Okay, fine, that might be getting a little dramatic, but that's what it felt like.

After a large breath, in which I summoned Aunt Lulu's calm bravado in the face of absolute ruin, I stopped tapping my foot. I peered beyond his shoulder back into the gym. Better to dance with him and get this conversation over with, so he didn't cause a scene. "Sure. Why not? Let's dance, Sir Jasper."

At first, he took my hand, gripping a little too tightly, so I jerked it away. "I can manage to walk inside. Thank you very much."

We strolled back inside through a sea of coattails and shimmering gowns to stand as if under a spotlight in the center of the dance floor. I saw immediately through his con—his attempt to reverse my lunchroom break up and show that I couldn't live without him or some nonsense like that.

After a couple minutes of dancing, he spoke in my ear. To anyone else it would look like the whisper of a happy couple, but anyone who knew me and knew him would know better.

"What were you thinking?" he asked, then tilted his head so his cheek grazed mine. Trust me, there was no swooning happening.

That was the wrong question to ask me. "There is something I've been thinking about this past year. Don't misunderstand me, I didn't spend hours contemplating this but I've often wondered why some of the male species, no one in particular, feels that moccasins are cool."

His hand tightened at my waist and his breath hissed against my ear.

I rambled on. "I mean, is the ability to wear this type of shoe in direct proportion to the size of one's ego? And if so, would this stretch to other nerd apparel like sci-fi T-shirts or pleated pants? It would make a great social experiment."

Jasper swayed a little faster, his shoulders tensing up under my fingers. The slow song ended and even though a faster rock song started, he didn't release his grip. We kept slow dancing as if no one else were around.

At that point, I should've known better than to push him farther. But let's face it. My night had been terrible, and it wasn't going to get any better. All the disappointment and frustration and hurt over the past year funneled into this one conversation.

"Or," I teased, "it would make a really great essay."

"Enough," he hissed, his voice taking on a dark tone as if he were the black knight. "You dared write a paper from my point of view that said stuff like that? You made me look like a complete jerk."

He tore into me, barely stopping for a breath. "You dared break up with me in the cafeteria? I went out of my way to ask you to the Valentine's dance after you walked through school in that ridiculous outfit. I did something nice for you, and I didn't have to."

Gee thanks. I thought back on Zeke waddling and crinkling his way into the lunchroom, dancing with me. "I wonder. Did you consider wearing the moccasins to prom? I bet you could've gotten away with it."

"And then you basically forced me to go to prom with you by pulling that ridiculous stunt with my family."

I plastered on a smile, my insides turning to mush and my knees feeling wobbly when I thought about Zeke. He went out of his way to try and get me to talk, to face whatever my inner demons were. I shook those thoughts off, and refocused on Jasper. "Oh, by the way. How is your family? I loved your mom. She was so nice. Did she get you started on the moccasins?"

Each time Jasper started in on me again, his voice went a little higher and got a little louder. Couples were forming around us, and they weren't dancing.

I thought about the look on Zeke's face when I basically said yes to Jasper that fateful day. Enough! I had to stop thinking about him. "Or maybe it was your dad. Maybe that taste in shoes runs on your dad's side."

He pushed me from his arms with disgust as if he couldn't handle being near me for one more second, and he didn't care anymore about pretenses.

"Enough about the shoes!" he roared. If anyone hadn't been paying attention, they were now. "Are you crazy?"

I kinda crumpled on the inside and split apart at the seams. Any Aunt Lulu I'd been channeling fled, and the night caught up with me: Zeke and Ava. The limo driving away without me. And the pink, twirly, glittery satin dress with the spaghetti straps. And my dreams crashing like falling stars.

He stepped real close, towering over me, his body shaking. I honestly don't think he would've hurt me, because he's not the abusive, violent kind of guy. His mom was too nice to raise a son like that.

"Get out," Jasper spit out, taking another step toward me, if that was possible.

Not many people have ever stuck up for me. I mean really defended my honor, even when I didn't deserve it. Jasper was getting ready to start in on me again, when the mannequin dressed in Carter's homemade chain mail crashed to the floor, the sword skittering across the floor.

"No. She's not leaving."

"She's staying right here."

"Stop being such a bully."

Jasper flipped around to Carter, Zeke and Michael standing shoulder to shoulder like they were the Knights of the Round Table.

Zeke was breathing heavily, the veins in his neck pulsing. He had fire in his eyes, the look of a guy who'd been there and back, the look of a guy who used to be a bad boy and knew how to deal with worst of them.

"Whatever guys. Enough," Jasper snarled. "She deserves it."

He couldn't even blink before Zeke's fist met his jaw. "When are you going to learn? Do you really want another black eye from me? Because I'd be more than happy to give a repeat performance."

My heart almost stopped, and a flush rose from my neck up to my face. That was Zeke? He'd punched Jasper after the party? It wasn't Michael? I stumbled back, the world spinning.

Jasper rushed Zeke with every ounce of football experience behind him, and they landed on the floor, a tangle of arms and legs and punches. Carter and Michael tried to pull Jasper off, but each time, he managed to break free. Girls shrieked and clutched their dates. The dates cheered the guys on. Mr. Troller danced around the edges of the wrestling match, trying to get in a word edgewise, trying to break up the fight before someone got killed.

Zeke's tough and all, but he didn't look like he was winning. And I didn't want any of these boys to get hurt. I grabbed the sword and whacked Jasper over the head with it.

"Stop!" I screamed. And I kept hitting him until finally, they all broke apart, their chests heaving, sweat and blood on their faces. "All of you, stop fighting." I pointed the tip of the sword at Jasper's face. "You will not hurt this boy. He's the only one who's ever tried to get to know me, and I will not have you messing with his face before I get a chance to kiss it. Now back off!"

Jasper took another step back but let out a little snort. Then the whispered giggles spread around me. That's all it took.

I spun around, facing all my classmates. "I might stretch the truth sometimes but so do all of you. Every time you spread a rumor without knowing if it's true, then you lie too." I whirled back to Jasper but was talking to everyone. "All I've done is barely kiss you. And yes I happened to overhear your little conversation with Michael outside the bathroom that night, and I was wearing a stupid shirt that wasn't mine, and I was hot and didn't want to cry in front of everyone, so I left. And that's why I wrote your paper on the wrong topic so you failed it."

Mr. Troller let out a little gasp.

Jasper's face grew fiery red and he spit out, "Hey, I was just trying to do as you asked or bribed me to do. You remember, don't you? You wanted to make Michael Greenwood jealous. Why? I have no clue."

Everyone started murmuring, gossip spreading like a forest fire on a dry, hot summer day. They'd never understand me. My arm with the sword lowered but when Zeke eased toward me I raised it again, my eyes blurry with tears and my throat aching. "Senior year was supposed to rock. And it sucked. Everything I did was an attempt to make this year the best of my life with friends, a boyfriend, and prom. But obviously that was impossible." Then I cracked myself up with a half laugh-half sob. "Prom impossible."

There was so much more I wanted to say, but it would've come from a place of pain, a private place that I wasn't ready to share, that I was barely ready to face myself, that I'd been ignoring all year.

That's when smoke billowed into the room, swirling in great clouds from the hallway. I knew right away it was a prank, the juniors copying our great smoke-out move from last year, the move that was the beginning of the end for me. But even though in my head I knew this, panic spread. Classmates screamed and rushed out of the gym-turned-castle and into the parking lot.

Through the thickening smoke, both Jasper and Zeke were led out by the scruffs of their necks. I stood amidst the chaos, numb and overwhelmed by the truths slamming against the walls of my heart, wanting freedom, wanting to be recognized.

I desperately needed to be alone. When I heard the sirens in the distance and had the sudden fear that I would somehow be blamed again, I raced out the side exit.

And I ran right into a wall—kinda. More like a cop.

CHAPTER 31

"IT WASN'T ME! I promise." I jumped back from the officer probably there to slap some cuffs on the guilty party. "This dress, this big poofy dress proves I'm innocent, because it's the underclassman who aren't wearing dresses who are the ones pulling pranks."

The cop raised an eyebrow and I could've sworn it was the same one who got a little cuff happy last year with me. "And why would I think you're guilty?"

"Oh, I don't know. Because cops like to find the wrongdoers so they can wrap up a case even if the person they think is guilty might not be the only guilty party. Ya know."

He crossed his arms and peered more intently at me as if weighing my innocence. "Actually, I don't know."

"Oh, right, of course." I laughed loud and high and waved a hand. "Well, I must be going. This smoky air is getting to me." I raced off but the heels and the dress made it hard to escape before he pulled me back.

"Do you know anything, miss?" he asked sternly.

"Absolutely nothing. Nada. Zero." I shrugged. "Like I said, I need to go."

He led me to the side of the building. "First, I'd like to ask you a few questions."

I walked several feet away, my heart in my throat, and my legs shaking. This couldn't be happening again. Before he could ask the first question his walkie talkie crackled and he talked a bunch of cop speech. I got the impression he was needed elsewhere. I held my breath, hoping, waiting.

He pointed a finger at me. "Wait right here. I'll be back in three minutes. And just in case you didn't know, fleeing the scene of a crime can be interpreted as guilt."

I saluted. "Yes, sir."

As soon as he moved inside, I took off toward the Porsche, but half way there I knew I couldn't drive it again, especially under emotional stress, so I rocketed around the parking lot with nowhere to go. It was filling up with people and cars, and more sirens were heard racing toward the scene to make sure there was no real danger.

That's when the gleaming white limo pulled up next to me. Carter popped out the driver's window. "Want a ride?"

I glanced around and then past the limo. "Where's the driver?"

He shrugged. "Smoking somewhere maybe. But he left the keys in the ignition."

I slid into the front seat and kept right on going, nudging him out. "I'm not letting you take part in this crime, so leave."

"What're you talking about?"

"The cops are looking for me, and I don't want you to be part of aiding and abetting and go to some Adventure Program this summer, so just stay behind. I'll take care of my own getaway."

He narrowed his eyes. "What did you do *this* year?"

I shot daggers at him and wished I still had the plastic sword. "I didn't do anything, and I wasn't the only one last year. Nobody else came clean."

"Huh?"

"Yup, that's right. Last year it wasn't just me. I was just the only one who got caught—wrong place wrong time—so now that you know the dirty gossip—leave!"

He opened the door to get out, but I pulled him into a hug first. "Thanks for sticking up for me in there." Then I dug in my purse for the keys to the Porsche. "Um, can you take care of this for me?"

"No prob." He stood outside, still in shock at the gleaming key in his hand. "You're amazing, sis. Crazy, but amazing."

"I know." Then I ripped out of the parking lot driving what felt like a three-mile long bus. When I peeked in the rear view mirror, the cop was in the parking lot looking at faces, looking for me. Too bad he wouldn't find me.

This wasn't about me not wanting to talk to the cop, because I was pretty sure I wouldn't be found guilty, but sometimes we're considered guilty until innocent and not the other way around.

I drove the dark streets, realizing I didn't look very inconspicuous. The evening was wearing on me and I needed time alone. I needed a lot of time to face that private place of pain I'd been ignoring for weeks. I needed a solo night, just me, myself, and I, because there were so many conflicting thoughts swirling inside my head, I didn't know what to do with them.

Finally, I pulled into Uncle Rudie's driveway, knowing I had to tell him his baby was okay, but the house was dark and no one was there. I tried the front door and the back door, but everything was locked. I walked around back and curled up on their swinging love seat in the yard.

I'm not sure how long I sat there, but it felt like eternity. The school, the fights, the smoke, the prom—it all faded and it was just me and the blanket of stars above me.

I thought about last spring and how in that moment of indecision I'd let Jules escape because of our pact. But was that my job? Was I being compassionate or being a fool?

I thought about Michael and how long I thought for sure he was the one, and then he did things that didn't live up to what I thought my soul mate should be. And is there such a thing as a soul mate, or did I completely make it up from movies and happily-ever-after books? I couldn't ignore the fact that he didn't really like me in that way. A soul mate connection is supposed to be reciprocal.

I thought about Jasper and how, for the second half of the year, I let him dictate my happiness and what I could and couldn't do. I lost a friend in Zeke, because Jasper controlled my life like I was the puppet and he held the strings. But I was the one who gave him that control, when I started writing his papers for a plan that never worked. Michael never batted an eye that I was "dating" the popular jock.

And then I was stuck.

I tried to think about Zeke, but all I could remember were all the times I didn't take our support group seriously, because I didn't think that he would understand. And then I remembered the look on his face when I chose Jasper that day in the cafeteria.

I thought about how badly I wanted a mug of hot chocolate, because the night was cooling off and my brain was fried and needed sugar to keep going, because I wasn't done thinking.

I thought about Aunt Lulu and the puffs of canary yellow tulle and crinoline and satin surrounding me and the ginormous flower attached to my shoulder, and that's when a sob broke though. All because of a dress. A pale pink shimmery satin spaghetti strap dress. One that Ava was wearing when it should've been mine. But I mean it was just a dress? Why was that so important to me? And why did I want to cry whenever I thought about it?

That mystery puzzled me. I knew it went deeper than that the dress was just plain awesome, and I would've looked hot, because I knew now that wearing the dress would not have fixed my mistakes. It wouldn't have prevented Jasper from being mad at me—I did that all on my own.

My thoughts chased each other in circles, but at some point, I couldn't handle trying to figure everything out. The answer floated nearby, taunting me, just out of reach. A fog had invaded my brain and covered the truth and the pain. I fell asleep, curled up on Aunt Lulu's swing.

***

THE FIRST THING THAT woke me up was a tongue. Hemingway whimpered, then barked. His paws were up on me, and he was kissing my face. I sat up and hugged him, trying to get my eyes to open. When I finally managed, the inky blackness hovered and dark shapes rushed at me.

With a scream, I toppled off the swing. "You stay away or my dog will attack. I know he looks young and inexperienced, but he's more than that, so you'd better back off my uncle's property before he hurts you. He loves me something fierce. Even though he's my brother's dog, he's really mine at heart, because I'm the one who takes him out to pee early in the morning and sometimes that's what counts. Who's there for you during the hard time and the small times—"

"Ma'am?"

"Back off, or I'll tell him to attack."

"Ma'am, it's the police. We were the ones who brought your dog."

I buried my face in Hemingway's neck. "I can't go through this again, Hem. I just can't." I looked up. "Can't you just pretend you didn't find me? I really need to talk to my uncle and aunt, and they should be back any second. In fact, I don't know why they took so long. Maybe you should see if they're stranded somewhere with a flat tire—"

"If you could come with us, miss."

I studied their built forms and long legs and wiggled my toes in my heels. "Think I could outrun you?"

"I wouldn't advise it, miss." It was the cop from the school, the one who'd asked me to stay and told me if I ran I'd look guilty. He'd found me.

"Do you have the heat on?"

"Yes, Ma'am."

The smaller one walked forward and helped me to my feet. I didn't have much fight left. I was cold and shivery and had blisters on my heels, and my heart felt raw and exposed.

Limping, I let him lead me to their cruiser. I could've run if I'd wanted to, and I'm pretty sure I could've had a chance if it weren't for the dress and the heels.

On the way to the station, I vaguely remember blabbing on about teen crime and asking how many years do teen criminals spend in juvie. But they didn't say much.

They didn't drive me to the station like I expected for taking off with the limo.

They brought me home.

CHAPTER 32

As I STOOD IN front of my door, it wasn't pitch black anymore, but it wasn't exactly morning, just this strange kind of lightness. Hemingway lay by my feet, faithful until the end, not heading inside or scratching at the door until I was ready to go inside.

The cops remained at the curbside, waiting for me to make my entrance and tell my parents I was off to the clink again. At least they were giving me that. I laid a hand flat against the wood. On the other side, in my living room, was my family. Dad, Mom, and Carter. Uncle Rudie, Aunt Lulu, and probably Jules.

I cracked open the door and slipped inside. My family sat with their backs to me, huddled on the couch. Aunt Lulu rubbed Mom's back in a gesture of caring I'd never seen. Jules was in a hushed conversation with my dad, and Carter strummed on his guitar. Tears rushed to my eyes because I was home with my family, imperfect and everything.

"Will you stop that darn playing," Dad said.

Mom gasped and fanned herself. Aunt Lulu bristled like a dog shaking off rain water. Jules snorted. I couldn't help but giggle while wiping away the tears.

Mom was the first one to see me. Her mouth dropped open and she squeezed Dad's hand. Then, one by one, they all realized I was there. It only took about two seconds of shock and awkward silence for them to all move toward me at once.

"I'm sorry!" I put up my hands like a shield. "Please don't—"

Any of my words were muffled by every person in my family trying to hug me at once. It was like I had scored the final touchdown in the homecoming game, and they couldn't get enough of me. During that hugfest, someone stepped on my toes, I swear my dress ripped, Uncle Rudie passed gas, and I heard several swears and accompanying gasps.

A strange feeling bubbled up inside.

That feeling swelled, choking me on the inside, and I couldn't hold back the rush of tears flooding my eyes. My breaths came out like a shotgun and I started hiccupping.

"She's having a panic attack!" Mom yelled, and everyone slowly backed off.

I stood there a bawling, hiccupping mess. "I'm sorry for everything this past year. Mom, I'm sorry I always get so dramatic on you, going on and on about stuff. I'm sorry I always disappoint and fail because I know how much you care—I mean really care—and I can't always live up to that. But...I'm me, and along with that come my nervous rambling and my impulsive decisions. I'm sorry I'm not who you want me to be, and I'm sure it's too late..."

Dad spoke. "I'm sure I speak for all of us when I say that you don't disappoint us, and we don't want you to be anyone but you."

The tears kept coming. "But you sent me to the Program, and you made me go to that support group, which by the way didn't work well, and you kept wanting me to be someone I'm not. I've tried, and I've had the worst year of my life. And senior year is supposed to be your best year, the pinnacle of your life, when you should get the guy of your dreams and have the perfect prom date and wear pink dresses." I crumpled over.

Mom led me over to the couch, her hand softly stroking mine. "We did not send you to the Adventure Program because you disappointed us or because we didn't love you, but after last spring, when the cops and the school got involved, we had to show them we were taking proactive steps. I thought you knew that."

"Stop!" Jules cried.

Everyone looked up because Jules is always the model of social perfection. Aunt Lulu twisted her hands and bit her lip.

Jules stood, trembling. "I can't take it any longer. You all have to know." She rushed to me and dropped in front of me. "I'm so sorry. I never...never...*never* should have let it get this far. I should've spoken up last summer, but I was too scared."

I wiped my tears. "You don't have to do this." But something inside me continued to swell as I saw the complete and utter brokenness on my cousin's face.

"Yes, I do." She took my hands in hers. "Cassidy, you are one of the bravest people I know. You know what you want and you go after it. You are you, and I love you for that. I pander to the trends and the popular crowd where you're brave enough to swim against the tide."

"I'm not sure if that's a compliment or not."

"It is. And it's time everyone knows it too." She faced our family. "It wasn't just Cassidy last spring who set up all the smoke machines at prom."

She grabbed me in a big hug and whispered, "I am so sorry."

Then she faced the family again. "It was me, too."

Something stabbed at my insides. This wasn't completely her fault. I didn't stick up for myself. I let someone else dictate my happiness.

"Jules?" Aunt Lulu trilled. "What are you trying to say?"

"Mom, I'm not perfect, and I can't be perfect. It was my idea to prank the senior prom, and like a coward I let Cassidy take all the blame. And I'm so sorry."

Everyone's face turned a tiny bit paler, but the truth bombs weren't done yet.

"No, it's not Jules's fault," I said.

Everyone looked at Jules and then at me.

"Well, is it or is it not true?" Dad asked.

"Well, it's true but I don't blame Jules anymore. I should've stuck up for myself. I should've told everyone what happened instead of accepting all the blame. *That's my fault.*"

I finally realized that if I was stuck wearing a poofy yellow dress with a ginormous flower on the side, then it was my fault. It wasn't Aunt Lulu's. I could've insisted on trying that perfect pale pink shimmery spaghetti strap dress. I see that now. If I got stuck at the Program or in a support group with Zeke, even though his crooked teeth and his smile and the way he cares about me—or used to—grew on me every day, then it was my fault.

Mom clapped her hands, calling everyone to attention. "There is a matter we need to discuss. Everyone please take a seat."

We did. I hung my head. This had to do with the Porsche. It had to. Except I didn't think everyone—or the police—would be so forgiving about grand auto theft.

"We have to clear up a few misunderstandings. First, Cassidy, dear. Where have you been all night?"

"Well, after prom, I went to Aunt Lulu's house and waited in the backyard in the swing...and then I fell asleep.

Hemingway found me." At the sound of his name he trotted over and lay at my feet.

"You didn't think to call? We've been worried sick all night after Jules told us about your little melt down at prom. You're not in trouble, but in the future, you need to let us know where you are. Understood?"

"Understood."

Mom straightened her back and a no-nonsense attitude came over her. Inside, I was secretly cheering her on even if she was about to send me to the Adventure Program again.

"And now, what is this nonsense about senior year being the pinnacle of your life and the year you find the perfect guy and have the perfect prom?"

"Well..." I looked to Carter and Jules for support, but they just shrugged. "After that it's all downhill, ya know?"

Aunt Lulu ruffled her body like she was a giant flamingo about to take flight. Then she snorted in a full-out piggy noise, so unlike Aunt Lulu that I almost giggled. "Cassidy, you've got to understand—"

"I'll take care of this, Lucille, if you don't mind." Mom looked back at me. Aunt Lulu sat back down a bit miffed, but listening. "High school is one of the hardest times of your life as you struggle with who you are and who you want to be. Never mind the added pressure of popularity, grades, and college to think about." Then she looked and incorporated Carter and Jules. "Your whole life is in front of you, and what kind of date you get for prom doesn't dictate how the rest of your life will go. Got it?"

We nodded. I think finally, we'd run out of words and apologies and truth telling.

"I've been working on this new song." Carter reached for his guitar.

"No!" we all said.

Dad stood. "I think it's time for tea and coffee and maybe some toast with jam and butter."

I looked at everyone and soaked in the peacefulness. "I guess I'd better go."

"Where on earth to?" Dad asked.

I nodded toward the outside. "The cops are waiting for me." Because I was guilty again. I stole the limo and Uncle Rudie's Porsche. Carter coughed and edged towards me. "I have one more thing I need to say. Uncle Rudie, it's about your Porsche."

"What about my Porsche?" A look of mild alarm spread across his face from the raised eyebrows to twitching nostrils.

"Well, I—"

"What she means to say is that she wishes she'd had the courage to ask you to take it to prom." Carter rushed over and clapped his arm around me while dragging me toward the window.

Uncle Rudie let out a big roar like that was the funniest thing he'd ever heard.

Carter whispered, "Long story but everything's as it should be. The Porsche is back in the garage. Uncle Rudie knows nothing. And I paid off the limo driver. He was just happy to have his limo back in one piece."

I blinked back tears. Carter had stood up for me and protected me, everything a twin brother should do. Even when I didn't deserve it, he'd covered my butt.

I laughed along with Uncle Rudie. "I know. Stupid idea." Then I turned back to Carter. "So the cops aren't here to arrest me or bring me in for questioning?"

He moved the curtain and peered out. "What cops?"

I smashed my face to the window. The cop car was gone. They'd been looking for me because everyone was worried. That feeling squeezed inside me again. My family loved me, and no matter what I did that would never change. They really loved me.

Someone knocked on the door. With Dad in the kitchen, Uncle Rudie strode over and opened it. He can be kind of intimidating when he wants to be, and it was like six in the morning.

"Yes," he boomed in a rather intimidating way.

"Is Cassidy home?"

CHAPTER 33

USUALLY I'M ALL UP for company, but at that moment I looked like Cinderella accidentally drank too much punch at the ball, and then her pumpkin carriage crashed, and she walked home with one slipper that didn't fit too well. My eyes had to be rimmed with red and probably bloodshot, and my hair, well, I hadn't looked in a mirror and didn't really want to. Plus, I was coming off an emotional tsunami of family bonding and self-realizations. Not the best time for company.

Jasper tried to step through the doorway, but Uncle Rudie puffed out his big belly. "State your purpose, young man."

I peeked around Uncle Rudie's shoulder.

"I'd like to talk with Cassidy, sir."

"State the nature of the talk." I couldn't see my uncle's face but I wouldn't want to be on the receiving end of his look. Jasper shifted and tried peeking around to find me. Uncle Rudie moved with him step for step. "I repeat, state the nature of the talk, young man."

At the sight of a good-looking youth, Aunt Lulu swished forward and gently laid her hand on my uncle's shoulder. "Maybe we should let Cassidy deal with this."

With a harrumph, Uncle Rudie, stepped aside, but when Jasper took a step in, he held out his arm. "You can talk to her from here."

Even though my uncle was being gruff and a bit like a troll, my heart swelled at the fact he was trying to protect me. I stepped forward and studied Jasper. A sheen of sweat lay on his face, like he was nervous about something.

With the support of my family behind me, I said, "Our partnership is officially over. You owe me nothing and I owe you nothing." Jasper wanted to say more, probably sick to his stomach at the thought of the trouble we could be in come Monday. "We'll deal with everything else at school."

"That's not why I'm here." He stammered out a few words before he spit out what he came to say. "I know I gave you a hard time the past few months, and I'm sorry about that." A look of wonder crossed over his face. "I've never had a girl stand up to me like that and, well, I just wanted to say sorry and I wish we could start over, because I'd ask you out on a real date." His face flushed a deep red, then he nodded. "That's all." Then he walked away.

Uncle Rudie turned and muttered, "Boys."

Aunt Lulu winked at me like a proud mama hen. Dad walked in with a tray of tea and buttered toast. We'd all just sat down and I'd wrapped my hands around the mug, when someone else knocked on the door.

"I'll take care of this." Uncle Rudie nodded to my dad, who was adding sugar to his tea, and then opened the door, puffing out his belly again. "State your purpose, young man."

"Is Cassidy home?" Michael asked.

I needed a moment. I closed my eyes and breathed deep. I'd waited all year—ALL YEAR—for this guy to stop by, to talk to me, to treat me like a friend. I'd convinced myself I was in love and went to extreme measures just to get him to notice me—all of which failed.

"Yes," Uncle Rudie stated.

Jules squeezed my hand. "Sweet revenge," she whispered. I squeezed her hand back.

"Could I see her?" Michael asked, then quickly added. "I have something of hers, I believe."

Uncle Rudie stepped aside. Michael searched all our faces until he found mine. His face lit up and he started babbling like some lame fountain in the heart of Italy, and I didn't even know if there were fountains in Italy.

"Those were some pretty awesome sword skills you had back there, and I noticed this got left behind. I thought you might like it to remember the night by. Sorry I never got the chance to drive you home, and I just wanted to make sure you were okay." He bit his lip and glanced at Uncle

Rudie before plunging forward. "Maybe we can hold a *Lord of the Rings* marathon movie night sometime this summer."

I stared blankly, mouth open, speechless.

Jules nudged me. "Looks like he's the one with stars in his eyes."

"Um, yeah, maybe," I finally said.

"Cool!" He smiled, his eyes twinkling a bit. "I'll talk to you soon." He handed the sword to Uncle Rudie then turned and walked away.

"Sword skills?" Mom asked, when we were all sitting again, sipping our now lukewarm tea and soggy toast.

I shrugged. "Don't ask."

There was another knock at the door.

Uncle Rudie huffed, because he hadn't even had a chance to sit down. He opened the door and sighed. "State your purpose."

Zeke eyed the sword still in Uncle Rudie's hand.

"I know how to use it, too," Uncle Rudie lied. "Now what do you want?"

"I wanted to dance with Cassidy at the prom, but with everything—I never got to."

"Cassidy?" Uncle Rudie asked without saying the words.

I sucked in a breath, and all the twisty feelings I'd been feeling toward this boy surged forward. Oh my, God, I couldn't see him looking like this. Like some lip gloss and mascara could help me now. I turned to Jules. "Help!"

Mom walked over and pulled me to my feet. "Remember what I said?"

I nodded. I remembered because at the time it seemed so contradictory to the truth. Basically, beauty doesn't come from perfect hair, makeup or the clothes we wear—even though it helps. And Mom had left me to figure out where true beauty does come from. Looking at my family, I finally knew. It came from loyalty and friendship and being there for one another and talking and listening and laughing. And it even came from all day shopping trips and poofy yellow dresses with ginormous flowers on the shoulder.

"It's okay, Uncle Rudie. You can let him in," I said, my voice a bit breathless as the twisty feeling turned into a small flutter.

Zeke stepped forward, a bit in awe of the circle of family surrounding me. He ran his hand through his hair, mussing it up even more, and I loved it.

I stepped forward. "I'd love to dance."

He met me, arms open. "This is kind of awkward," he whispered, after his arms were around me.

"I know. Just pretend they aren't there."

A second later, the first strains of Love Story strummed in the background. I heard a couple of sniffles and sighs from swooning women. My dad slurped his now cold tea while Jules and Aunt Lulu pulled the coffee table to the side. Every time I moved, the flower growing off my shoulder crinkled and brushed his face.

I broke away. "Hold on a second." I took hold of the flower and yanked at it until it ripped off. "No offense, Aunt Lulu."

"None taken. Carry on."

Zeke chuckled and held me close again. This time I stepped even closer, enveloped in his warmth and let my cheek rest against his. There was so much I needed to talk to him about. Everything he'd tried to get me to share last summer and through all our support group sessions. He didn't know I needed to stick up for myself more or that I needed a dose of self-confidence.

I whispered, "We have so much to talk about. You're my friend and I barely know anything about you like whether you like peanut butter or jelly or your favorite movie or your favorite color or what toppings you like on your pizza or if you have a pet cat."

He didn't say anything, just smiled.

And I definitely fell into an all out swoon.

"Okay, you two," Aunt Lulu stated. "Enough chatting and more dancing. You can talk all you want tomorrow, but you're ruining the romance for the rest of us."

He smiled, revealing his crooked teeth. He kissed my cheek, a light feathery touch that made me melt into his arms. "Didn't you mention something at the dance about kissing me?" he whispered.

My heart slammed against my chest. "I might've, maybe, possibly said—"

His lips met mine. They were soft and warm and everything delicious. A shiver ran through me.

The women sighed and Dad cleared his throat. A clear *Back off from my daughter*.

With a happy feeling fluttering about in my chest, I rested my head in the crook of Zeke's shoulder and let out a swoon-filled sigh.

Sometimes we have to wait to find our own love story, even if it's only the beginning and even if it doesn't turn out to be forever. I'd just have to wait and see.

The End

About Laura

Laura Pauling is the author of the exciting young adult *Circle of Spies Series* and the time travel mystery, *Heist*. She writes to entertain and experience a great story...and be able to work in her pajamas and slippers. *Prom Impossible* is her newest YA romantic comedy, published as of May of 2014. To keep up on her new releases check out her website at http://laurapauling.com and sign up for her newsletter so you don't miss out!

CPSIA information can be obtained at www.ICGtesting.com
Printed in the USA
BVOW06s2218091215

429910BV00021B/107/P